SAW.

HOWARD BAKER

MAINSTREAM
PUBLISHING

EDINBURGH AND LONDON

First published in Great Britain in 1999 by
MAINSTREAM PUBLISHING COMPANY (EDINBURGH) LTD
7 Albany Street
Edinburgh EH1 3UG

Reprinted 2001

ISBN 1 84018 223 7

A catalogue record for this book is available from the British Library

Typeset in Garamond
Printed and bound in Great Britain by Cox & Wyman Ltd

'These long-haired, mentally unstable, petty little sawdust Caesars seem to find courage, like rats, by hunting only in packs . . .'

Dr George Simpson, Margate Court Chairman, May 1964

With thanks to Graham Coombs-Hoar at
Cooms Contemporary, artist Danny
Cuming, Simon Bradshaw at Newsquest
(Sussex) Ltd, Pete Morris at Hulton Getty,
Louise Taylor at the *New Statesman* and
Lynda, for her love and understanding.

PROLOGUE

When Marilyn Wisheart packed her shoulder bag that sunny June morning, placing her maths and French homework carefully apart from the sandwiches to avoid stray margarine soiling her work, she had no idea that later that day, at 4.35 p.m. to be exact, she would be raped in front of twenty-seven males by someone who, up until then, she had only ever come face to face with in her wilder moments of teenage fantasy.

Not that sex was anything new to her at the tender age of seventeen – she had, according to school folklore, already miscarried, and was therefore branded a slag – but whether she deserved to be shagged in such a fashion by Kenser Donnelly, an ex-pupil of the school who sometimes came back to the metalwork rooms in the evenings to make parts for his motorbike, was open to frequent and often passionate discussion.

Kenser Donnelly, twenty-two years old and a motorbike freak, was not one of us. For a start, he was dirty; his greasy black hair was Elvis and his style was, well, Gene Vincent, Cochrane, Haley, a fifties throwback. A degenerate escapee from *The Wild Ones*. His jeans were oily and torn, his leather jacket studded and scuffed, and around both wrists he sported studded-leather bands as a signal to the rest of the world that he wasn't to be taken lightly.

Worse, in every town and village from Scotland to the south coast lived another Kenser, and every one of these

Kensers had a gang, a small army of greasers, who ruled the roost unchallenged, like barbarians in a foreign land. Where they came from, or why they existed, was a mystery – maybe being born during the years of war had something to do with it; perhaps the noise had damaged their fathers' sperm, or warped the fragile eggs in their mothers' ovaries – but who in their right mind would want to live like a beast, with sweat and grime and stinking greasy hair and rotting teeth as the mark of their breed?

Like most of my generation, I hated and feared them, but we were still too young to do much about it.

The school itself was an experiment, designed, as they put it, to allow kids the greatest chance to excel and prove themselves by offering the most modern facilities and up-to-date methods of teaching available, but in fact it was little more than a vast and unpoliceable pile where the basest of teenage instincts were allowed to flourish without check. As a pupil in it, you either sank or swam – equality and opportunity didn't count. From the start, those of us that formed the rebellious hardcore realised that it was the same old turkey in a different cage and we reacted by dismissing this trendy and patronising concept of education from our minds.

But I mention the rape of Marilyn Wisheart purely because the events that afternoon reinforced in a big way a strange and uncontrollable mood that was growing in my seventeen-year-old mind, a mind already influenced by aggressive war-battered parents, poverty, street violence, endless social double standards and my own ideas of reality which seemed at odds with everything my elders believed; few were those I trusted, and, like thousands of other kids waiting on the sidelines, I was ready to smash my way out of the mould that had for too long shaped the destruction of our own predecessors.

The accepted view, of course, is that the events which occurred during the early and mid sixties were little other than hooliganism and civil unrest – the 'steadily growing indiscipline of the young' and 'a deliberately cultivated form of modern wickedness', according to the Chairman of Hastings Magistrates. But for once, perhaps, it might be worth considering them through the eyes of a teenage male, a young man who actually took part in this social revolution – for that's what it was – instead of through the eyes of those entirely unqualified to do the job. For many and varied reasons, history has a habit of pouring from the wrong mouths, and as the past also has an undeniable habit of shaping the future, where possible those who pronounce on it should be those who have valid experience.

Everything you read about here is true, and many of you will recognise the various incidents and anecdotes as they arise, but for reasons that will become obvious I have taken the liberty of disguising most of the characters, times and places to avoid any comeback to myself or any other person who might or might not have been involved.

This, therefore, is an entirely false yet enigmatically very real account of the Mod and Rocker days of the sixties.

Have fun.

ONE

AN ENEMY OF SOCIETY

Way across the roundabout, on the other side of the road from the school, Kenser Donnelly lounged on his old BSA motorbike. He listened to the pips as they sounded for the end of the day, and the uproar that went with it as two thousand kids scraped their chairs across the floor and rushed for the doors and home. Two thousand kids, that is, less six of us who were waiting behind for Marilyn Wisheart, who had discreetly let it be known that she was up for a bit of harmless molestation after school.

There were girls who liked to be waited for and girls who didn't, and those who did came down to the cloakrooms in the basement where the older boys gathered. Marilyn Wisheart was a frequent visitor, as was Jane Royce, and Sandra Veness, and Monica Fisher, and Christine Sharp, and Pam Drysdale . . . the list goes on. And it was all very innocent. Sometimes, if they were up for it, a bra might come off, or Goggles – a strange kid with a hearing aid and a long, thin knob – would masturbate (which the girls liked watching, incidentally, despite their weak protests), but until this day, without a single exception, these liaisons were little other than innocent attempts to relieve mounting adolescent sexual frustration.

Dinger, a close friend of mine from the same estate, the youngest of a family of market traders, was dancing about between the coat racks singing a ska sound we'd heard in La Discothèque in Soho, where we went every weekend:

'Madness, madness, they call it madness . . .
Madness, madness, they call it madness . . .'

Anyone would have thought he was black, the way he was dancing: shifting about, bobbing up and down, swishing his long, red suede coat from side to side. But Duffy, who wasn't one of our lot, had just lit a Consulate and was scared he might attract attention with the noise, and said so.

Dinger stopped dancing and stared at him. 'Fuck off, Duffy. If I want to sing, I'll fucking sing, all right? If you don't like it, fuck off.' He liked to fight, which was one of the few things he could do well; as far as education was concerned, he was a complete no-hoper, failing all his exams year after year. I mean, everybody passed something at some stage – but not Dinger. Now, in this last year, the school would be glad to see the back of him.

He carried on singing:

'Madness, madness, they call it madness . . .
Madness, madness, they call it madness . . .
I'm about to explain, that someone is using his brain . . .
Madness, madness, they call it madness . . .'

Mac was dark – not black, but dark – and he was really deep-down unhappy about it, convinced by years of taunting as a kid that he was impure, but could he pull the birds or what? Everywhere we went, he pulled. In fact he was a bit of a let-down on that score because he would rather pull a bird than get up to a bit of roguery, given the choice, but he was a sound mate and knew how to dress, getting stacks of money from his mum to keep his wardrobe full of nice gear like handmade shoes, mohair suits, tab-collar shirts, coloured leather jackets and long suede coats.

I had a full-length suede too, a lovely cream one which I'd nicked from a shop in Shaftesbury Avenue, but it was too hard to keep clean and very identifiable, so I'd done a deal with Mac, who was going to swap it for a maroon leather, then sell it on to his sister's boyfriend, who he hated.

In our world, clothes came first, followed by drugs, music and sex, because without the right clothes your rating was nil, and without the drugs your mind became open to all sorts of undesirable influences like the law and you became boring, and without the music – the right music – your finger just wasn't on the pulse. In theory – or fantasy – sex naturally followed the other three.

We didn't know it at the time, but two other ingredients, violence and murder, were about to enter the equation in a big way, big enough to make the headlines on and off for the next couple of years. But the future was the last thing on our minds that afternoon in those dark basement cloakrooms.

Dinger was peaking now:

'I'm gonna walk right over you . . .
Madness, madness, they call it gladness . . .'

'Sssshh!' It was Duffy again. He'd arranged the rendezvous with Marilyn. 'Here she comes! Don't let her see you all!' He was worried she might back out if she saw there were six of us waiting.

There was a moment's silence as we followed his gaze, broken suddenly by Dinger again, who was trying to wind Duffy up.

'Can I fuck her, Duffy?'

Everyone knew that Duffy saw her as his own, although she was anybody's, and Dinger, who still had a few old-fashioned but confused morals lingering in his head, resented this on the grounds that if he felt that way about her he should be protecting her and not encouraging these social gatherings.

'You wouldn't know which end to start.'

It was Mac this time, but no offence was taken as he made up the third part of our trio of friendship.

But Duffy sniggered.

'Right,' hissed Dinger. With a speed that comes only with natural talent, he kicked Duffy in the groin hard enough to knock him back against the wall, where he squatted, clutching his balls, his mouth wide open, unable to utter a sound. Dinger considered for an instant whether to follow up with another to the head, but instead turned away to peer through the coat racks at Marilyn Wisheart, who was now only about twenty yards away, her arms folded casually across her breasts as she approached.

She wasn't a great beauty facially, being inclined to outbreaks of acne, but she had the figure and legs of a star, which caused a great deal of disturbance among the pubescent males of our school, which included just about everyone.

Drawing level with the coat racks, she stopped and stared. 'Where's Duffy?' she asked. There was a defiance, a challenge in her voice, and we moved forward out of the gloom.

'I kicked him in the bollocks,' explained Dinger. He nodded towards Duffy's huddled figure.

'What did you do that for?'

'He said he wasn't going to let me get your tits out.'

'That's got nothing to do with him anyway,' she said indignantly.

At this clear signal we moved in and within seconds her blouse and bra were off, but somehow the word had got around and instead of being left alone to enjoy ourselves we were joined by a score of others who suddenly flooded through into the cloakroom, keen to get a piece of the action. Feeling suddenly threatened, Marilyn began to resist and struggled to escape, pleading that she'd had enough and wanted to go home, but the mob was out of control and she was hoisted aloft and carried like an offering for sacrifice to a nearby classroom, where she was stripped and spreadeagled on a table for examination.

At this point an alarm bell rang in my head. Something made me look up – and I saw, there by the door, the black-leather-clad figure of Kenser Donnelly.

The clock above his head said 4.35.

Like Moses parting the waves, he cleared a path through the crowd to the table, and stood staring at Marilyn Wisheart's naked body like an animal. Breathing heavily, he seized her by the legs and, encouraged by some of the crowd who were now chanting 'Go on, Kenser', he dragged her towards him, undid his fly and pulled out his ugly dick.

Through the crowd I heard her pleading weakly with him to stop: 'Please don't, please don't . . .'

But he wasn't listening. Expressionless as a snake, he forced the thing inside her as she, pinned down by the other boys, stared at the French-room ceiling, gritting her teeth and clenching her fists in pain and desperation.

Until that point I'd felt nothing but lustful curiosity about the whole thing. Sex, as far as my own experience went, had been confined to messy encounters under difficult circumstances and a desperate biology lesson given by a teacher strait-jacketed by embarrassment, so a demonstration wasn't entirely unwelcome. But the inhuman attitude of the mob towards the girl stirred the mud at the bottom of my personal pond and I didn't like it one little bit.

Dinger, meanwhile, had moved away with a strange look in his eyes and Mac, sensing a problem, nodded to me. We followed and asked quietly, to avoid being overheard, what was bothering him.

'I don't know,' he said, throwing his head back in defiance, 'This is out of order.'

'Let's go, then, come on,' said Mac.

'It's just that cunt, Kenser . . .'

This could be dangerous if Dinger stayed true to form and lost his rag. Kenser was a notorious hardman; someone would almost certainly get badly hurt if there was a violent confrontation – and the odds were stacked against us.

Suddenly there was a commotion behind and we turned to see Kenser pushing his way back through the crowd, fastening the zip in his grubby jeans. Seeing us standing apart from the crowd, he hesitated, picking up on our mood, and looked aggressively at me – I have this naturally insolent look which tends to get me into trouble. 'Something wrong?' he asked, half smiling.

How I would have loved to have decked him with one punch, spat in his face, stabbed him in the eye with a bayonet or just said 'Yeah,' with a note of defiance in my voice, 'what are you gonna fuckin' do about it?', but I shit out, and hated myself for it. 'No,' I said tamely, 'it's just that you're older . . . it don't seem right, that's all.'

Not only did I hate myself then, but I suddenly hated Kenser Donnelly with a violence I'd never felt before towards anyone: he'd forced me to hate myself, and that was a terrible thing to do. I was no match for him, and he also knew I wasn't daft enough to take a beating for the sake of appearances.

Encouraged by a few jeers from the mob behind him, who were hoping to see a bit of bloodshed as well as rape, he leaned forward, pushing his leering, greasy face into mine close enough for me to be able to smell his fruity bubblegum breath. 'Do you want to make something of it then?' he asked.

All the frustration that comes with still being a child, a child on the brink of manhood, flooded in, and all I could say was 'No' as defiantly as possible without running the risk of provoking him into physical violence.

He grinned and swaggered out of the room.

Marilyn Wisheart was dressing herself behind us as the crowd, apparently satisfied with the performance, dispersed to tell the rest of the world that they'd seen her being shagged.

'You all right, Marilyn?' asked Mac. We felt badly uncomfortable, like we'd let her down in a big way.

'No,' she whispered with tears in her eyes, buttoning her blouse. 'Where's my bag? I want to go home.'

I think we all grew up then.

The last day at school came and went through a vivid filter of purple hearts – triangular amphetamine pills – and alcohol. Dinger threw up in afternoon assembly; I challenged the Deputy Head to a fight – I knew he was knocking off a gym mistress on the sly – when he started going on about the lack of morals of modern youth; and Mac shagged Sue Creasey in the broom cupboard while everyone sang 'Dear Lord and Father of mankind, forgive our foolish ways'.

Rounded up by a posse of teachers, we were escorted grinning like clowns to old Davidson's office, where he went on and on about respect and loyalty to the school as we looked around the room trying to avoid each other's eyes in case we laughed in his face. We were finally denounced as enemies of society and expelled. At that,

Mac, staring deadpan at the wall behind Davidson, politely said, 'Thank you sir,' and Dinger, unable to contain himself any longer, farted aloud and burst into laughter.

And there it all ended.

After years of crap what did I have to show for it? Not much. Not in the eyes of society, anyway.

Three poxy GCEs.

'Out of the eater came forth meat, and out of the strong came forth sweetness.'
Judges xiv. 14

'. . . and we may take this famous verse as an indication that sometimes the end justifies the means; that sometimes there must be destruction, the breaking down of old barriers, for there to be forward movement. And sometimes that destruction cannot be seen at the time for what it truly is, the work of Almighty God.'

Davidson
Afternoon Assembly, June 1963

I've always thought how funny it is that there's this separation, this dividing line between me and society; well, maybe I'm being naïve about it, but I always thought I was society, or at least a little part of it.

But old Davidson said I was an 'enemy of society'.

I was also a failure 'in the eyes of society' according to the slag in the magistrate's court when I got done for thieving, so what exactly does that mean?

Logically, it means I must be apart from it, otherwise society would be condemning itself, wouldn't it? And the society I'm referring to doesn't do that.

So if I'm apart from it, what am I?

I must be another society, or a little part of another society. Get my meaning?

In which case, who's to say who's right and who's wrong? After all, here we have two societies with different values.

One thing's for sure: I know what I think, and what I believe.

So you in that other society who think you know better, who sit in judgement, trying to tell me how to lead my life, do you know what I think? I think that it's not me, it's you who are the enemies of my society.

So fuck you.

And if we had a show of hands on this one just to see how many there are on each side, you might just get a nasty surprise.

Build your barricades while you can, because your time is nearly up.

We've got you sussed.

FUCK YOU.

Yours truly,

Tommy Spitz, June 1963

TWO

THE WEST END

It's a warm Friday night in early summer, just after dark, and I'm strolling along Old Compton Street towards Wardour Street with Dinger and Mac, aimless, but looking as if we're going somewhere – it's the way you do it, like you're one of the boys who's one of the main geezers around Soho. It's important to look the part.

Dinger's still got his red suede coat and Mac his green leather, but I've got the new maroon leather with the long back pleat from Mac and I'm feeling pretty smart because it matches my pink strides and black polo shirt with the red-edged collar which I got my mother to pay for, bless her.

The only downer is that we've got no loot, so the search is on for someone to roll, and every geezer we pass we're giving the eyeball to see if he looks like a soft touch.

So far, we've done half a dozen purple hearts each that we blagged off one of Mac's old birds we saw outside the Scene, but we need a lot more to last us through until dawn, otherwise it'll be an early comedown which fucks up the rest of the night and the next day. Dinger's already grinding his jaws – he gets a bit strange on speed and isn't really cut out for it – but underneath it all he's a bit of a home boy, you know what I mean, with a mum and dad he cares for and brothers and stuff, but it makes him weaker, not stronger. Don't get me wrong, he looks the part with his cropped sandy hair and flat nose, and he's well tasty when it comes to a scrap – in fact he always loses his rag and goes over the top – but he's soft when it comes to other things, like that Marilyn Wisheart who got shagged by Kenser Donnelly. He still hasn't got over it. He reckons that if he don't kill Kenser, he'll get his brother Vince to do it.

I've heard about Vince.

But whatever. It's a strong family and I wouldn't like to cross any of them. Especially Vince.

My family are different from that. For a start, I'm the only child, a sort of 'one's enough' statement, and my mother's spent half her life trying to turn me into something she wants me to be, whereas my old man would rather I didn't exist at all. A mean and moody bastard, he hates the fact that his lady's got someone else in her life to love and never lets the chance slip by to put the boot in in some nasty underhand way that my mother won't notice. I used to think a lot of him once but I've seen through him. Good luck to the man, it's his life. But I don't care about all that shit because the sooner I can get away from the pair of them the better. They just cramp my style. What I need is a flat like Frankie, who's got one in D'Arblay Street where he keeps his little bird Norma on the game part-time for the spare cash. It makes all the difference to their lifestyle – you should see the blinding clothes he wears, all handmade gear, real quality stuff, and I get on all right with him, although a lot of people don't, seeing as he's a nutter.

I just love speed. Makes you feel real good. Makes you talk a lot. Mix it with booze and you're fucking invincible.

On the other side of the road is a drunken sailor, would you believe, leaning up against the corner of Dean Street, looking like one of them wooden toys which collapse when you press the button underneath.

21

'Come on,' says Dinger, stepping straight out in front of a car. 'Let's go and see if the man would like to donate to our Benny Violent society.'

Ignoring the curses of the car driver who looks a bit big to argue with, we cross the road and approach the sailor, Dinger in command as he seems to regard this as his one. 'Oi, cunt. You got any money?' he says. Nothing like the direct approach.

The sailor drops his hand from the wall and straightens up, revealing his full height. And he isn't as drunken as he looks, either, he's just relaxed and taking in the scenery. 'What?' he laughs. 'You want money from me?'

'We've lost our fare home,' explains Dinger aggressively when he realises the man's going to be no pushover.

The sailor's still grinning and fearless, an unnerving attitude when you're considering a bit of nastiness. 'Young lads like you could easy make money round here – you got nice little bums; go and find yourself a punter.'

'D'you fancy my arse then? I've heard all about you sailors,' sneers Dinger.

The sailor laughs out loud, and I swear you could hear him down the other end of Old Compton Street. 'I'd rather shag a dead pig,' he says.

'Fuck off. Just give us some money, all right. A couple of pound'll do.'

This was going to be a bit tricky. Dinger didn't want to lose face in front of us. It's all about losing face – everything's about losing face in our world.

The sailor shoves his hand in his pocket and for a silly moment we all think he's going to oblige, but he pulls out a penny and throws it on the floor at our feet, telling us to go away and buy some sweets. We glance at each other and are on the brink of jumping on him when an even bigger sailor comes out of the shadows doing up his flies, putting paid to any ideas we might have had of teaching him a lesson for being cheeky. As casually as possible, we walk away.

Dinger looks back. 'Fuckin' queers!' he shouts, and starts to prance around in the middle of the road singing, 'All the nice boys love a sailor, all the nice boys love a dick . . .' – until the big one throws an empty beer bottle at us and some bouncers come out from the Samson and Delilah strip club to see what all the noise is about.

Just down from the Crown and Two Chairmen, where some of the moneyed bunch drink when they're slumming it, we hang around in the shadows waiting for one of them to come out, whiling away the time talking about nothing as the speed zips through our brains, making us feel confident. When you're planning a bit of skulduggery or violence, you have to be careful you don't get into a benevolent frame of mind when the amphetamine takes hold, otherwise you could end up being nice to people.

After a little while, a tall, dignified, white-haired gentleman in a pin-stripe suit, carrying an umbrella, comes out, staggers just a little bit, pulls himself together and begins walking unsteadily towards Soho Square. He stops to check his pockets, then carries on walking, reassured that he hasn't left his wallet behind – makes you wonder how these people survive at all, sending out signals like that for all the world to see.

Buttoning his coat, Mac says he'll run round the block to cut him off and ask for the time – there's never anyone in charge on these jobs, we just work instinctively as a team – and lopes off, while Dinger and I stalk him from behind, having had a quick look around to make sure nobody else is about.

As usual, Dinger's getting overexcited. 'I bet he's loaded,' he whispers. 'He looks like a rich cunt.'

'Just keep an eye out for the Old Bill.'

'I want his watch . . .'

'Just the notes, just the notes . . . what's the matter with you?' You have to keep him in check with the odd harsh word every now and again, otherwise he loses it.

Dinger falls silent. He isn't too bright with the villainy side of things either. His heart's in it, all right, but he has difficulty seeing even one step ahead, except perhaps when he's kicking someone in the face, and the thought of getting captured and having to talk his way out hasn't crossed his mind. The last thing anyone needs is hard evidence against them – like an identifiable watch. As it is, an excess of spare cash'll be hard enough for a seventeen-year-old waster to explain.

'There's Mac!' he hisses, happy to change the subject.

Up ahead, we can see Mac crossing the road to ask our man the time, and as they meet we attack, running swiftly up behind just as he raises his arm to look at his watch. I catch him with a hard punch to the side of the head and Dinger follows with another, and after a pitiful attempt at resistance, crying out, 'I say, I say, this isn't cricket you know,' down he goes in a flurry of fists and boots, cracking his head on the edge of the wall for good measure. We're over him like dogs then, rifling his pockets, plundering his wallet, pulling out wads of notes, all the while keeping an eye out for witnesses or Old Bill, but if there are any, they are keeping well out of the way.

There's more than enough to see us through the night like rich men. Enough to buy hundreds of pills and swan around the West End in taxis all night if need be, going from club to club. I could take Sandy Jones to the Flamingo and impress her with the details of how we rolled the geezer and maybe get a bit of the other. Or better still we could get a room somewhere and wait until the pills wear off . . .

But Dinger's not quite finished; he pulls the man's black Oxford shoes off and throws them into the shadows. I look about, just wanting to get away, worried that someone might show. 'What the fuck are you doing?' I grumble. Mac stands there, mouth wide open, his eyes popping out of his head in astonishment. It's at times like this the spade in him rises to the surface.

'Making sure he don't follow us,' Dinger replies earnestly. He then pulls the poor man's trousers off – after a fierce struggle with the braces – and stuffs them inside his coat.

'He's not going to follow us! Are you losing your mind?' cries Mac.

Try as we do to appear to be three law-abiding citizens as we emerge once again into the bustle of Old Compton Street, none of us can keep a straight face and we cry with laughter as we run all the way to the Coffee Anne.

The Coffee Anne, a basement coffee bar which everyone's currently using, is packed as usual, and we have no problem sorting out four hundred dexedrine – yellow amphetamine pills; a hundred now, three hundred later – and sixty hearts for immediate personal use, which we wash down on the spot with Coke to make them faster-acting and easier to swallow.

Frankie's there with his tasty blonde Norma, who must be off duty, but he says I can have her at cut price if I want because we're mates. She just laughs and looks even tastier, and I don't know whether he's joking or not, but all I can think about is the pox. Dinger had said she's got syphilis and that it can't be cured and that you went mad with it – so I've fallen in love again but don't dare touch her. I'm weird like that; I fall in love every day with different sorts and I find girls with venereal disease repulsive yet very attractive. Work that one out.

And the speed keeps kicking in very nicely thank you.

The world is wonderful and the Stones are playing on the jukebox and everything is just perfect. Everyone is unbelievably beautiful and kindhearted and I'm so happy to be with my friends in the vibrant atmosphere of this beautiful basement bar.

Everyone's talking at once about everything and pretending to listen but only hearing what they want and I think I'm talking about Margate or Brighton next bank holiday and Chislehurst Caves next week where there's going to be a ruck with the motorbike boys who go down there and Dinger says if he sees Kenser Donnelly he's going to kill him and Frankie says not to worry because he's going tooled up and he'll make sure no one comes to any harm because he really loves his mates and we all agree that we're all best mates and then some geezer some fucking bumpkin from out of town starts shouting at a beautiful little sort accusing her of taking his money and Frankie tells him to shut up because we're all having a lovely time but the geezer just won't leave it out so Frankie hits him with a glass ashtray and carves 'F' in his face with it and we have to get out quick before the Old Bill get there blue flashing lights laughter sirens and bells running down dark alleyways full of amazing energy flying spinning round lamp-posts stopping for a piss snogging with Norma running again can you catch a dose by kissing? Who fucking cares anyway and lights and slow down now, out into Gerrard Street and on towards Wardour Street and La Discothèque. We are the King Bees . . .

Up up up the red stairs into the coloured world of pounding sounds and spinning lights and bodies, love comes on strong and I find Sandy waiting with Gail and some others from the estate looking for pills and I can supply free of charge because I am one very smooth geezer and suddenly everyone wants to know me. Sandy is hang-

ing on like a small starry-eyed child keen to be associated
but I know that she's like that anyway with anyone who can
come across with the goods. Feed me feed me feed me is
Sandy, always going where the going is good but she is
pretty and sharp as a knife and story has it that she shags. I
fingered her last week and she didn't smell bad like some,
she smelled kind of sweet, makes you want to go back for
more and I'd really like to come in her but my knob's like a
jelly bean now. She wants to lay on one of the mattresses
that are placed around the edge of the darkened room
where, in the middle, some very smart geezers from Romford are dancing real pretty to James Brown's 'Night Train'
and she's already giving them the glad eye, but that's Sandy.
Good job I'm not the jealous type – not with her anyway.
Now she's starting to come up on the speed and I can't get
a word in edgeways.

'So anyway,' she says, 'I went down the Rye with Gail
and Linda and that Paul with the green suede you know the
one I mean the one whose mother's got a bad leg or
something and I saw this girl there who'd nicked my suede
at that party in Leytonstone you know the one so I said oi
you fucking slag that's my suede you've got on there and
you know what she tried to say? She tried to say it was her
sister's fucking cow . . .'

Her sister's cow?

'You know what I mean you cunt she said it belonged to
her sister . . . oooh I see what you mean, her sister's cow, her
sister's fucking cow . . . aaaahhaa . . .'

Then she goes into fits of laughter and starts choking,
screaming 'her sister's cow!' between gasps, all her black eye
make-up running down her cheeks, then she gets up and
runs to the bog still laughing and I wonder what else she's
on because you don't usually get hysterical on speed.

She comes back quieter now but still a bit giggly,

laughing at the laughing, and says she wants to go outside for a breath of air but I know what it is she really wants and start to get worried because my dick's too small.

Out out out through the smoke and bubblegum and mint and leather smells, through the sound and into the peace and cool of the stairwell where she leads the way down but halfway down we pass a couple of black geezers with two black girls and I instantly fall in love with one of them who is so beautiful. Our eyes search each other and linger inside and I know she likes me then a voice says 'you coming up or what?' and both of the black geezers are looking down at me and her looking at each other and a voice from below says 'you coming down or what?' and the black girl looks down at Sandy who's turned into an ugly slag and carries on climbing the stairs with lovely long legs and a tight bum.

But she looks back and smiles.

Sandy's arm in mine and I don't fancy her for a while and we go into dark alley just up from La Discothèque where she puts her hand inside my trousers pulls willy about and says I should have guessed we'll have to leave it finger me instead so she comes with a little grunt and I get an aching finger then she goes back in and I make excuses and go off sniffing my finger for a walk in the big wonderful London lights talking to strangers loving them all drop some more pills and I feel so fucking good everyone's beginning to look at me so I get paranoid and dart down a dark street with whores like a crocodile in a long suede coat and go into a tiny café for a drink but everyone in there is extremely strange and behaving very oddly like slow-motion water buffalo and when I look at them they look away so I fuck off quick and run straight into Frankie who's been doing some business somewhere but he won't say what not that I care because I'm beginning to think lairy now. Listen Frankie I don't want to know your business right I don't give a fuck what you're getting up to I got enough on my own plate right now know what I mean fuck I'm buzzing now and could easily kill someone and I'm wondering whether it should be Frankie or not which would give a nice little boost to my growing reputation and he sees the madness in my eyes and says he thinks I'm great and suddenly I've stepped up the ladder to Nutterland.

Walk around a bit walk around a bit walk around a bit then back into La Discothèque up the red stairs show your wrist stamp and into the pounding room again love the music and feel safe Dinger's there Mac's there Sandy's not there but what do I care and dancing real nice in the middle of the room is very tasty black wondergirl with her friends so I join in feeling pretty good now. Gypsy woman, can I hold your hand? . . . Come on now, gypsy woman, can I hold your hand? My name's Sherri mine's Tommy pleased to meet you this is my brother Neville and *his* friend Leroy and basically I'm unattached she says without speaking the last bit but Leroy doesn't like this because he badly wants to get across Sherri and he looks threatening but I'm way beyond his reach in another starry world . . . anyway I'd kill him so fuck off and don't look at me like that all right . . .

A slow number and she agrees to press herself against my pounding heart and I wonder what it's like to go out with, to put your knob inside, a black girl. She smells a bit different, sort of jungly, all flowers and tigers and I can feel myself losing grip and about to do something silly which would be dangerous and even my dead knob is beginning to twitch again. Then it's Dinger shoving his silly face into mine and asking if I'm coming down the Coffee Anne again or what because we've got to pick the dubes up and Sherri seizes the moment and pulls gently away saying that I should go with my friend and I see Leroy growling behind

her and realise she is being smart. I whisper see you in the
Flamingo in an hour I'll pay and Georgie Fame's playing
and she says maybe.

'What'd you pull me away for, you cunt, couldn't you see I
was going to pull that black chick?'

'Fuck off, I was just trying to stop you from getting a
spear in the back from that black *geezer*. Anyway, all I
wanted to say was that Sandy's fucked off with one of them
blokes from Romford.'

'Yeah, and?'

'Just thought you wanted to know.'

'Why would I want to know that?'

'Well I don't fucking know, do I?'

'What do you mean you don't know, you cunt?'

'Don't know . . .'

'Fuck's sake, Dinger.' Change the subject quick. He's
blocked. 'You got any money left?'

'A couple of quid.'

'Give us a pound.'

'Fuck's sake, Tommy. Where's all yours?'

'Spent it.'

'What on?'

'Pills. Drinks. Fags.'

'Stroll on. Here's a pound.'

'Ta.'

Wash more pills down with sweet milky coffee, walk
around a bit, meet Frankie again and Dinger goes off with
him to roll someone. I go to the Flamingo, upstairs from
the Whisky-a-go-go, and scan the room for wondrous black
girl but she isn't there. Gail's there with a bloke from Cable
Street who looks extremely dodgy and I sit and talk to them
as I come up again and he begins to look better and then
we become best mates.

Just as I'm about to give up and go looking for Mac, she comes in, spots me and comes straight over.

'Hi!' She talks a bit Americanish for some reason, but it's nice, and in the better light of the Flamingo I can make out her form without looking too obvious about it. Apart from being a good-looker boat-race like, her figure is as near perfect as you can get. 'I like your coat,' she adds, as if seeing it for the first time, and I like her even more. She's wearing a tiny black tight-fitting dress and very powerful bright red lipstick.

'I like your dress.'

'Thank you. It's nice in here.'

'What, inside that dress? No, sorry, I'm just being silly.'

She smiles. 'You are, aren't you.'

'I do get silly sometimes . . . First time you been?' I'm doing my very best not to appear blocked, in case she's one of these holy blacks.

'Yeah. My brother talks about it but I don't come out very often. Tonight's a bit of a treat really.'

'Why's that?'

'It's my dad – he's so strict.' She laughs a lovely little gasping laugh. 'He thinks I'm still a little girl.'

'No, I mean what's the treat?'

'Oh, nothing really, he just relented. He's got to start letting go sometime, I suppose.' She's the same height as me and slender, which is different, because normally I go out with girls who are a bit smaller than me to make me feel bigger.

Then another rush starts and I say do you fancy a dance and Georgie Fame comes on and I drip sweat all over the floor while he plays 'Watermelon Man' and I say I know I've only known her for a couple of hours but I'm crazy about her and will she go out with me and she whispers hotly in my ear that she doesn't know and my heart hits the floor but she says she'll think about it but she has to leave now or her brother might come looking for her and he could get annoyed and if he says anything to Dad she might not be able to come out for another month.

My head swims like crazy. Do I get a kiss?

A brush of those red lips.

And she's gone.

* * *

Back in La Discothèque, the music stopped just as the comedown started, just as the first terrifying crack of blue-grey dawn glared from behind the heavy maroon velvet curtains and the morning starlings began to scream a warning of impending misery and daylight. Eyes crusty and mouths foul, we poured under protest from the warm, red corridor into the strange half-light of cold dawn to face the promise of another day.

A bad speed comedown can be suicidal stuff, especially if you're alone, so we stuck together like pygmies in a dying neon rainforest and scurried to the underground public lavatories in Broadwick Street for a wash and tidy-up. From there we drifted in small groups towards Mick's Café in Fleet Street, one of the few places open at that hour where you could get something to drink; eating didn't come into it.

And as we walked along the Strand, the new sun came out to scour our ravaged brains with blinding fingers of light.

Inside Mick's were the hardcore of the nightclubbing crowd, everyone on a comedown bar one or two who still had pills left, but to me it was always better to take the comedown rather than prolong the agony, as you knew that sooner or later it would sneak up and get you in a big way.

It was always easier in the long run to cope with it on your own terms if you could work it that way. Anyway, I reasoned that once you'd done your bit of paying back for enjoying yourself too much, once your body had recovered from that onslaught, you could start again with another.

Casualties from excess speed were a lot less than some people made out. The most frequent were new drug-takers who took far too many for some reason or other, usually ignorance, unaware that those who dropped thirty or forty or more at a time had already built up a decent tolerance. For them it usually ended up with a quick trip to the hospital for pumping out and a telling-off, and rapid promotion to the league of idiots – which is a bit unfair, really, when all you're trying to do is enjoy yourself. But then life can be, can't it?

After a long period of speed and no sleep – say three or four days – you might have the Horrors creep up on you, a scary state of psychosis with hallucination and strong paranoia. And, naturally enough, kids being as vicious as they are, until you'd had them you weren't taken that seriously as a drug user. It wasn't unknown either for some people to try faking it rather than risk the real thing, but most of these were deficient characters who were unable to impress others by the usual means. These tended to need psychiatric treatment or steady jobs and mortgages as they got older.

From time to time, you might see someone collapse into a fit and degenerate into something monstrous, something sub-human writhing in a pool of piss and grinding their teeth; but when that happened you left them alone to get on with it, the philosophy being that if you took the drugs you took the consequences. In a way this was cool, because it taught everyone to take responsibility for themselves, knowing that no one else was going to bail them out if things went wrong.

Berwick Street market was where Vince, Dinger's big brother, had his fruit and veg stall, and that morning, still unable to account for the cash and pills we'd obviously squandered, Dinger suggested we pay him a visit on the off chance that he might be in one of his flush moods and drop us a couple of quid. So, paying out the last of our money for the teas and a packet of chewing gum, we set out back up Fleet Street towards Soho just as the first big red buses of the day began looking for passengers to avoid.

As I've already said, rumour had it that Vince was a bit of a criminal, and he looked and sounded the part. But if the truth be known, at that time I didn't really understand what a real villain was, just as I didn't know much about the big wide world out there beyond my own mind. I never dreamed for a moment just how ruthless and terrifying a real villain could be – or that in but a short while I would find out for myself – so it was with a confidence born entirely of ignorance that I first met him, and I think he took a shine to me.

He had a cheery manner that was reassuring and welcomed both of us with what seemed to be genuine warmth – but his affection for his little brother was quite plain to see.

'How you going, boys?' he beamed. He was in his early thirties, well-built and with a short college-boy hairstyle, like Perry Como. 'What are you doing out this time of the morning – shit the bed or something?'

Dinger grabbed an apple from the stall, disturbing the display, and offered one to me. 'No, we've been up La Discothèque.'

Carefully Vince restacked the tumbled apples. 'You'll get scabies going to those dives,' he muttered. 'Does mother know where you are?'

'She thinks I'm staying at Tommy's.'

Vince looked at me. 'And I suppose your mother thinks you're at his. You're boys, you are. What if the law gives you a pull? Then what?'

'We're old enough to be out,' argued Dinger.

'And old enough to keep swallowing them pills . . .'

'What do you mean?' protested Dinger.

'Eyes like the wrong end of a twelve-bore is what I mean. You look like a pair of Little Owls.' He looked over to a fellow stall-holder. 'Oi Billy! Look at these two herberts. Don't you reckon they look like they've escaped from the owl house at London Zoo?'

'Monkey house more like,' came the reply.

Dinger continued. 'Give us a couple of quid, Vince. We spent all our money last night and we're hungry.'

Without a word Vince put his hand in his pocket and gave him a fiver. 'Get me a large tea with three sugars, and keep the change. I want it back, all right?'

We rushed off before he could change his mind, bought him his tea, then disappeared before he could think of finding something else for us to do, across Wardour Street and into St Anne's Court, where we knew another little café. A fiver! Vince had to be rich. I nearly got a job as a building-site labourer and they were only offering fifteen quid a week.

It was by now promising to be a hot day and the comedown wasn't too bad, just ominous and vaguely depressing, but Dinger had a little surprise in store: a bag of purple hearts which he'd extorted from a young clubber on the grounds that they were bad for him.

'When he asked why, I said because if you don't give them to me I'll jump all over your head.'

'You crafty fucker! You should've said.'

'I didn't want everyone else to see them. Then I put them in my inside pocket and forgot about them.'

We swallowed a handful each and washed them down with tea, and slowly the world became a better place – the comedown would have to wait until later.

'You know what I've been thinking?' I said, feeling confidence rushing back in.

'No.'

'I've been thinking that we're going to need some cash for next weekend. I could do with some new gear as well.'

'A fiver's not enough.'

'What time is it?' I asked.

Dinger looked up at the clock behind me on the wall, which I hadn't noticed. 'Twenty-five to eleven.'

I spun round and stared hard at it. Five to seven, it said. And I was thinking of getting into a bit of mischief with this person? Oh yeah, I could just imagine it – meet you there at . . . or, be right outside with the getaway car at . . . or, if I don't show by . . .

'The big hand's on the eleven,' I said, 'and the little hand's on the seven. It's five to seven, not fucking twenty-five to eleven. It's early in the morning, not nearly dinnertime.'

'What about it?'

I gave up. 'If we go to Cheapside, there's a nice little shop down there with one old geezer inside who sets up the window about half eight every morning. I've been watching it for weeks . . .' – I was lying; I'd seen the old bloke doing his window once – '. . . and there's no one about on Saturday mornings. All we do is tie up the door handle so he can't get out to have a go at us, and smash the window.'

'He'll call the Old Bill.'

'Yeah, but we'll be miles away on the underground before they turn up.'

Dinger thought hard for a second or two. 'What sort of shop is it?'

'What sort of shop is it?' I couldn't believe him. 'It's a pie and mash shop. What'd you think it is?'

Dinger's jaw dropped. 'Pie and mash? Don't be a cunt. What sort of shop is it?'

'A fucking jeweller's, what do you think it is?'

Poor Dinger. He could be so thick he made the rest of us look brilliant, and sometimes I worried about him: I had the feeling that one day his failure to understand the simplest things that stared him in the face would lead to his undoing.

Cheapside was deserted, as I'd thought it would be, not a soul to be seen in any direction, and there but a few steps away was the jeweller's, its windows already laid out in full display. The only inconvenience had been carrying the rock from outside St Paul's to the scene of the crime, and it had left a nasty mark on my strides, but so what? I'd soon be flush enough to buy a new pair.

Dinger lashed up the door handles to the shop with string we'd found in some rubbish outside a stationer's shop, then stood back as I heaved the rock through the window.

Whether we were both a bit jumpy from pills and lack of sleep or whether the weekend peacefulness of the city exaggerated it I don't know, but the crash of breaking glass was so loud that we both bolted as soon as the window caved in, only to realise after fifty yards or so that we were running from nothing and that nobody had come out to see what all the noise was about. We stopped and walked warily back like innocent passers-by.

Dinger looked at the shattered window and shook his head. 'Just look at that!' he exclaimed loud enough for the old shopkeeper, who was bleating like a nanny goat and rattling at the doors, to hear. 'Who could have done a thing like that? Someone could easily take all this jewellery.'

Following Dinger's lead, I said aloud that we'd better take it down the police station for safekeeping. Quickly we filled our pockets with gold rings, diamond bracelets, gold chains and watches, until the rattling at the door stopped and we knew it was time to run.

Off we went down Cheapside again, back towards St Paul's, and on into the maze of little streets that run between Ludgate Hill and Queen Victoria Street, stopping for a breather and a smoke inside a Post Office building where we redistributed the loot between pockets to make it appear less obvious. Then we set out again across Queen Victoria Street to Blackfriars for the underground and safety. We'd pulled it off.

All we had to do now was sell the stuff to Fagin – our nickname – in Brick Lane, who we knew would try to pay as little as possible.

We started by offering the man – a skinny Armenian who looked like he'd just stepped out of *Oliver Twist* – just one piece, a gold bracelet covered with diamonds.

'They're spinels,' he said, eyeing them casually, trying us out to see just how stupid we might be.

'No they're not, they're real,' I said.

Not thinking again, Dinger said, 'They're real, all right, it said so.'

'What said so?' asked Fagin, looking up at us. 'You boys know I don't buy bent gear.'

'Don't listen to him, he's got a fever – keeps seeing and hearing things,' I said. 'This was left to me by my aunt, God rest her soul.' I crossed myself and tried to look pious.

He squinted again at the bracelet, then peered at it through an eyeglass. 'Not very good quality – I'll give you twelve pounds, that's it,' he said finally, grumbling to himself. We accepted his offer, knowing that we didn't have much choice in the matter, but as he counted out the money, the thought did cross my mind to knock him on the head and clean out the till; the trouble was, we'd have had every murderer in town looking for us after that and then there'd be nowhere to sell bent gear, so I dropped the idea.

'All right,' I said, now trying to look businesslike. 'Do you want any more like this?'

'Just bring it round, boys,' he said. 'Bring it around and I'll see what I can do.'

Dinger nudged me. 'What do you reckon then?' he asked with a wink. 'Should we show him the rest or take it down the pawn shop? Twelve quid ain't much, is it?'

I looked at Fagin and the drip on the end of his nose. 'Do we get a good price, or do we go to the pawn shop?'

'You know I'll always look after you boys,' he whined.

We dumped the contents of our pockets on the counter.

He gasped with open delight. 'My god, my god,' he said, chuckling. 'You had a very nice auntie, didn't you?'

After being told how difficult it would be to sell such undesirable stuff and how much of a favour he was doing us and how he would be lucky to make anything and how he'd just bought in a load like it for a lot less and how the gold price had dropped and how much of a risk he was taking, we came away with just under five hundred pounds for the lot. Not bad for a morning's work, despite one of the rings alone being marked up in the shop for more than that. But what was the option? You can't expect realistic prices from fences even if your goods are kosher because they've got so much bent gear coming through the door all day long from the likes of us they'd be fools to pay proper prices to straight punters. And a straight dealer would have called the law.

THREE

CHISLEHURST CAVES

'You look like a fucking poof!' The words of my father when he set eyes on my newly bleached French crop with shaved parting.

The pale-green straight-down silk strides riding three inches above maroon suede shoes and black socks left him silent, and I half expected him to lash out, but he just walked away in disgust. Then there was the striped Madras cotton jacket from Cecil Gees. And the dark-green knitted silk shirt from Krantz. Fuck. Did I look the business or what?

And I'd been measured for a silver/black Tonik mohair suit, slapping down fifty per cent on it. A slightly waisted, three-button, centre-vent, horn-buttoned, buttonholes real, straight-down strides, mean bit of schmutter to turn the dollies' heads.

And I'd scored a thousand blues, which I kept in a dried-milk tin under the bed, enough to keep me blocked for a month if I fancied a short-cut to the nut-house.

The big night at Chislehurst Caves finally arrived. The word had gone around and hundreds of kids from all over London and the suburbs were pouring into the area by train, bus, car and the odd scooter. Scores of Rockers were there, clustered in gangs around their bikes and doing their best to look frightening, but the mood was noticeably different as they seemed for the first time to be uneasy, aware maybe of the sheer weight of opposition that was arriving. Crowds of kids entirely undaunted, in fact attracted, by the motorbike boys' bad reputation were swarming full of confidence into the caves, intent on having a good time at anyone's expense; and the fact that many of them were speeding out of their brains and apparently fearless must have caused these bikers to wonder what breed of animal they were up against.

Chislehurst Caves was a twenty-two-mile maze of man-made chalk tunnelling, and the entire extent of it was left open for those who felt so inclined to wander about in, instead of having to listen to the bands that played in separate caverns each out of earshot yet within easy walking distance of each other. Once you'd paid to get in, that was it, you could do what you liked. There was little or no control and the bouncers stayed by the entrance minding their own business.

Once inside, there was a hundred-yard walk to the first cavern which housed the wilder rock bands – the main territory of the bikers – and it was there that we'd all planned to congregate in a show of strength.

At first there was nothing to hear but the sound of muted footsteps and chatter as we walked along the main entrance tunnel, but gradually a faint reverberation in the distance could just be made out. It grew louder and louder until we turned the corner into an almost solid wall of sound.

Across a sea of black leather jackets I could make out Sandy with Gail and Frankie and a few others standing by the stage. All around the outside of the crowd were groups of flashy kids, some I recognised from the West End, standing out in clean and colourful contrast to the dark, seething mass in the middle. Until then, the tribal thing hadn't really started and we still just about tolerated each other's company, with the Rockers administering little

41

kickings and beatings here and there, but the time for a big change had come and everybody knew it.

Frankie saw us and nodded across the crowd. Sandy waved, and we began shouldering our way through the heaving mass centred around a circle of bikers who were pushing and pulling, arms linked, in and out like a filthy black orifice, to the manic and aggressive beat of the group, the Wild Angels, who seemed intent on supercharging the hot air with violence.

I could see that Frankie was blocked as soon as our eyes met, his jaw grinding mechanically on a tiny piece of gum, his eyes rolling about, big, black and dangerous.

'Tommy, Tommy, I've been looking for you,' cried Sandy above the din. 'Where've you been?'

'Just got here. Fucking mad, ain't it?' I looked at Frankie. 'What's happening?'

'Later,' he said. 'It's all happening later. You tooled up?'

'No, why, should I be?'

Dinger butted in, pointing to his feet and clenching his fist. 'I've got these, these'll do.'

With a mad leer, Frankie pulled back his coat to show us a wicked-looking carving knife hanging in the lining. 'Just in case,' he said.

Unable to talk much above the noise coming from the stage, we stood around for a while weighing up the crowd but felt too on edge to hang around waiting, so we decided to wander about and regroup at around ten o'clock. As we were leaving, Sandy grabbed my arm and said she wanted to go exploring.

The jazz cave was more civilised, filled with intellectuals: beats, their big-titted birds, teachers, philosophers, poets and other tossers who didn't pose a threat. I downed another dozen blues with a bottle of Coke to boost the twenty I'd done in the station lavatory which didn't seem to be getting me off as quickly as usual. Perhaps it was the feeling running around in my gut that something horrible was about to happen, or maybe it was just that I'd been doing too many lately and my natural resistance was high, but I couldn't get into the swing of things.

Sandy, smiling and full of herself, was the opposite. 'I love these trad jazz bands – the Green Man at Blackheath's supposed to be good, so's the Mitre, but I never really liked them until I saw Chris Barber play. It was fantastic how he got the crowd going . . .'

'Out the door . . .' Mods don't dig trad jazz, daddyo.

'Don't be silly, no, you can get a really good atmosphere in some jazz clubs; d'you know they do weekends and boat trips across to France on the *Daffodil* with jazz and blues, sounds like a right laugh, someone got drowned last time, we'll have to go, d'you fancy that? I do.'

'Where did you get the pills from?' I asked, trying to break the flow of the one-way conversation. Did I fancy jazz on a boat? Silly cow.

'Frankie's mate Steve from Hackney gave them to me, he's really nice, you know him, he's got the light-blue leather – you haven't taken any, have you?'

She's so up her own arse she didn't even see me swallow the pills.

'I like it when you're straight – when you're blocked you go a bit funny. D'you want a chewing gum?' She rummaged about in her bag and found a stick of gum. 'Here,' she said. 'Let's go for a walk.'

* * *

Here she goes again; now she wants a cuddle, thinking I'm not blocked. What someone needs to invent is speed that gives you a hard on. Or maybe not, thinking about it.

So off we go, into the chalk tunnels with a lighted candle until we find a little unoccupied cave and start snogging standing up. I'm massaging her tits, trying to work up some enthusiasm, but if anything the speed's coming on stronger now – vicious fucking bastard that it is – and my lust hits a new low, driving my willy into reverse just as her searching fingers make contact.

She laughs scornfully and pushes me away. 'Ha, you *are* blocked. What's the point of saying you're not when you are? It's not as if you're going to be able to hide it.'

'I didn't say I wasn't – you did.'

'You could have said something, instead of letting me make a fool of myself.'

I like that one – her making a fool of herself. For fuck's sake, I've come out for a good time and now I'm squabbling with some fucking bird I don't even fancy any more who's got the needle because I won't – can't – fuck her. And now the speed's kicking in real strong like it's got a delayed fucking reaction. 'Look,' I say, rapidly gaining vast, huge fucking amounts of confidence. 'You wanted to screw. I didn't, all right? Maybe if you keep your mouth shut a bit more, you might learn something, now fuck off.' And I do a moody walk-off number, half expecting her to come running after me like they do in films, but when I reach the corner and glance back I realise that she has the only candle and is walking away in the opposite direction with it – so I have to run back and walk with her until we reach civilisation.

Blowing out the candle, she turns and looks me in the eye. 'D'you want to go out with me or not?'

I hesitate. 'I don't know,' I say truthfully. I really hate hurting her, but maybe I'm kidding myself.

'Well I do,' she says. 'As far as I'm concerned it's over.' Then she walks away with her silly little nose in the air.

Childish stuff – who could get the chuck in first. But I still like her.

So I think of Sherri and feel good again – if only she could see me now in this crazy place. It's good to have someone you fancy in your mind who might be thinking about you. Makes you feel strong – and I was going to need it.

Comfortably speeding and locked inside my head now, I pace back to the jazz cave to find someone to talk to, maybe a nice beatnik girl with a rich mummy and daddy, but get cornered instead by a lefty wanker who sees me as good conversion material. Funnily enough, after a bit I get on to his wavelength and tend to agree with a lot of what he's saying, but then you can when you're blocked. He keeps going on about inequality and the greed of our leaders being the bane of the working class and how we are in chains and how we should unite and overcome them, which I more or less agree with, and I tell him about motorbike boys and how they are bullying fuckers and how we are going to sort them all out, and he says that it is destructive for the working class to fight among itself and that we should work together in the common cause. Then he says he's managed to get a powerful union together at university and I tell him he's a two-timing fake who knows nothing about the working class because true workers wouldn't lower themselves by arse-licking around at university even if they could, which they couldn't. Working-class people are just that, I say: people who have to work or find money somehow every day of their lives to eat, not ponce about at university preaching about workers' rights. Then I walk away and leave him because I'm feeling unbelievably sure of myself.

Ten o'clock and the rock cavern is vibrating to 'Three Steps to Heaven'. All around the sides our lot are looking right edgy, waiting for something to happen, when Dinger bursts through the crowd looking anxious.

'Tommy, Tommy, you seen your bird?'

'Sandy, yeah, why?'

'What, lately?'

'Half an hour ago, why? What is it with you, keeping reporting back on her? She's not my bird anyway.'

'That's all right then.'

The way he says it hits me in the guts. Although I don't really want to go out with her any more, the thought of her being shagged by someone else makes me feel sick – she could at least show a tiny bit of respect for our short relationship. So I ask why it's 'all right then'.

'She's gone off with Kenser Donnelly.'

* * *

There are times in your life when you've no choice but to hang on to your emotions, times when no matter how confused, hateful, sick, disgusted and hurt you might feel, you have no choice other than to act cool while seeing red, mainly because short of going insane and making a complete cunt of yourself, there's nothing else you can do. You just have to bide your time until the moment comes when you can let off steam somewhere without damaging the friends who happen to be closest to you at the time, so I tried to put the vision of him shagging her out of my mind.

'Here he comes now.' It was Dinger's voice again, coming through the red haze in my brain.

Kenser was pushing his way back into the middle of the crowd towards his stinking pals, and I'm sure he looked over and grinned. A few seconds later Sandy showed, her neat little crop all ruffled, the make-up on her face smudged. Our eyes met for an instant, then she sniffed and turned away, unaware that the back of her coat was covered in chalk. Fucking little scrubber. How could she let a filthy biker put his hands all over her? I saw him in my mind shagging Marilyn Wisheart, then saw Sandy in her place enjoying it.

If anyone had said earlier that it was going to be me who started a war against the Rockers, I'd have enjoyed the compliment before admitting that I couldn't imagine how. But who can predict the future when blind rage takes the upper hand?

Dinger knew what was coming – he had that intense, innocent look on his face he gets before doing something rash.

'Here we go,' I said, and shoved my way into the middle of the leather jackets, ignoring the growls of outrage as I defiled their sacred territory. There was an unexpected moment as I came face to face with Kenser Donnelly when I saw fear in his eyes that made me hate him even more, and I punched him in the mouth as hard as I could, knocking him back into the crowd. A roar went up as the place exploded and everyone started fighting and throwing bottles. I felt an explosion in my head and saw stars as Kenser came back with a punch, and then another, but I kept my cool and fought back, striking home with several good blows to his face. With confidence mounting prematurely, I began to feel he wasn't all he was made out to be, but, suddenly changing style, he began clawing my face with his dirty fingernails and kicking and biting, and I began to feel pain as the blows from his hob-nailed boots struck home. Shoved together by the brawling mass, he clamped his fingers around my throat and I knew then that I was in serious trouble unless I could somehow throw him off. Within seconds I was gasping for air as he tried to throttle the life from me, squeezing those thick, oily fingers

47

as hard as he could, and I felt the strength draining from my legs, making it hard to kick back with any effect. Jaw set and staring into my eyes with a strange look of malicious concentration, he increased the pressure to finish me off.

But a strange thing happened – he suddenly appeared to change his mind.

With an expression of surprise on his face he let go, then looked down to his side, felt around his back and stared at his hand, which was covered with blood. 'I've been stabbed,' he gasped, as I sucked in huge draughts of air to regain my strength.

Behind him I saw Frankie disappearing into the crowd.

Was Kenser expecting mercy – or an intermission while he went and got himself patched up? A few seconds before he'd been trying to kill me, and I was still scared and mad, so I punched him in his frightened face as hard as I could, again and again, until he went down. I laid into him with my feet, kicking and kicking and kicking, trying to make his horrible vision disappear, until Mac pulled me off, shouting that the Old Bill were coming, and we ran out into the night.

FOUR

THE BATTLES BEGIN

By chance, I fell into a job as a general runabout in a strip club in St Anne's Court — it's funny how things go right when you're on a high — and I spent a couple of weeks in the early summer surrounded by the sort of older girls young men would talk about dying for.

The bloke who took me on was a Greek called Toni, a wiry little guy who seemed to take to me straight away. 'Come in, come in,' he said, 'I need a nice strong young man to help me look after the girls and keep the place tidy.'

As I had only been passing, trying to catch the eye of the girl who worked next door in the hairdresser's, imagine how I felt being offered such a prestigious job. Beats labouring any day. I shook his hand enthusiastically, tried to appear as employable as possible and was shown in.

Although still only mid-morning there were already a couple of girls hanging around, but when I asked what time the show started Toni explained that they had two bedsits above the club where they took paying clients, and he offered to provide one of them free of charge as long as I didn't mind him being there at the time. This was a new one on me and I politely declined, laughing it off as a great Soho-type joke, but I made up my mind instead to handle the girl situation in my own way, preferably when he wasn't about.

Every afternoon the show started and went on into the early hours of the following morning, non-stop, six girls in rotation, dancing to a set musical routine based mainly on Jimmy Smith's *Walk on the Wild Side* album, and I had to sweep up, run errands for the girls, make tea, be on hand for any rough punters, fetch orders from the local shops and generally be Toni's best mate. 'You be my friend – I look after you, okay?' Sometimes, if the girls saw him being friendly, they sniggered and made suggestive remarks, but it all passed over my head. Other times he asked if I fancied a bath and offered to take me down to the public baths where we could have one together, and I still didn't cotton on, being unaware that homosexuality was anything other than a twisted joke, so poor Toni fell cow-eyed in love with me, thinking I was just playing hard to get, entirely unaware that he was flirting with an up-and-coming psychopath.

One day I was poking around in one of the rooms upstairs where the girls did their thing, thinking that such a moody room overlooking all the Soho rooftops might suit me, when Nicole, a so-called French artiste, came in. She came from Clapham, as it happened, and was only a couple of years older than me, but she looked about thirty with all her make-up on.

She asked what I was doing in the room and if she could come in, so I told her I was just tidying up and putting things away. Without a second thought she began taking off her day clothes in preparation for her act, hanging each item neatly in the wardrobe until she stood there naked, trying to make up her mind which set of stage underwear to put on.

'I suppose undressing in front of geezers comes naturally now, does it?' I asked, feeling as if I had to say something.

She looked up. 'Only when I'm on stage. I wouldn't carry on like this normally.' She laughed.

'I'm sorry,' I said, suddenly feeling embarrassed. 'I didn't think. I'll go.'

'No, it's all right, darling,' she said. 'You boys don't worry me. As long as you don't mind, I don't.'

I didn't know whether to take that as a compliment or an insult, and I wasn't sure what she meant by 'you boys', so I asked.

She stopped and stared for a few seconds, then gave me a lovely cheeky smile. 'You're not, though, are you! I said you wasn't.'

'Not what?'

She explained. 'Usually Toni's boys are queer – the girls prefer it that way. And the way you dress, well . . .' She eyed me up and down, taking in the lilac slacks and pink John Stephen shirt.

So that was it.

Here was a dawning revelation – if you wore pretty clothes and hair, you had to be queer. And queer meant homosexual. Someone who shagged other blokes.

I tried to laugh it off without showing that I was a bit shocked. I know my old man had said that I looked like a fucking poof, and I'd expect that of him, but to imagine that the rest of the world might also see me as one – just because of my style of dress – was shattering. I thought everyone saw me as a toughie.

But on the other hand, I suddenly thought, why not confuse people? It could be useful . . . after all, Nicole was still standing there naked in front of me. That certainly wouldn't have happened if she'd realised what I would have liked to do to her.

But I think the sexual nature of the job and the circumstances of our meeting might have unbalanced my mind. 'Shall I prove I'm not . . .' I asked, as if it were the most natural thing in the world, '. . . do you fancy a screw?'

I shocked myself. I'd never been this direct before, having been raised by people who believed that sex was 'rude'. Usually there was a recognised approach, a build-up, some sort of pretence at love to make it appear all right and to make the girl feel comfortable, which led on to kissing, and then feeling up if you were in luck. But putting yourself on the line was a new approach to me, and I was suddenly nervous after I'd said it in case she went mad and accused me of being disgusting. I could even lose my job.

But instead she surprised me by being reasonable: 'You don't have to prove anything to me, Tommy. I think I know where you're at. If you're offering to take me out for a drink after work, you're on.'

And it all might have happened except that later that afternoon Toni came on strong and I head-butted him in the face and kicked him senseless, leaving him lying on the landing where I'd been sweeping up while chewing over in my mind exactly what Nicole had meant earlier. Fucking queer? Not me. I had no choice but to run – but not before I'd cleared out his cash-box to help rebuild my image – and had to give St Anne's Court a wide berth for a while.

I saw Nicole in Wardour Street a few weeks later and crossed the road to talk to her, hoping that I could get a date, but all she said was, 'Go away, you're nasty,' and clattered off on her stilettos.

Other people's stated observations can have a powerful effect on you, and it wasn't the first time I'd been put down as 'nasty'. When I was seven, a woman who paid my mother a pittance for doing her housework – a woman who was also very genteel and an upstanding member of the local community – called me 'nasty' for being too disruptive at her kid's Christmas party; made it clear to everyone that I was only there on sufferance as I was her cleaner's son; gave me a third-rate present from the Christmas tree after initially forgetting me altogether; and banned me from playing with her son again as I was considered to be a bad influence on him.

I knew even at that age it was because I was from a poorer family, a family lower down the social scale, that I'd been singled out – if I'd been the offspring of her husband's boss I'd have been fêted as 'energetic' and 'full of potential' instead. Believe me, if there's one thing kids recognise, it's injustice, and I soon learned that there were plenty of dodgy people out there ready, willing and able to destroy you if you didn't fit into their scheme of things.

Things didn't get much better. I was expelled from cubs at the age of nine, again for being 'nasty' – for getting even with the bullying son of a local teacher two years older and a lot bigger than me during a game of British Bulldog, when I'd kicked him in the head. A few weeks later, using a homemade catapult, I smashed the glass covering of an advert for Sunny Whitstable in a train carriage, was split on by a friend and went to court.

And then I was hauled before the court again and branded a hooligan by a pompous and condescending magistrate for borrowing an old lamp from someone's unattended bike. There was even talk of sending me to a remand home for juvenile delinquents. I love all the terms they use. They asked my old man if I was out of control and I thought my time was up, but he told them not to worry and said he would sort me out (mainly because if I went inside it would have destroyed my mother). Then he sulked and refused to talk to me for a month.

In class our form teacher, who had been asked to provide a confidential social report to the court, decried me publicly as a social misfit to be avoided and did his best to turn everyone against me. In fact, it was from here on that my reputation began to grow; but for him I would have crawled under a stone then and got on with learning something, happy to be left alone.

Anyway. Big deal. Childish misdemeanours exaggerated by adults. And an ill-meaning teacher who actually did me far more good than harm.

As you sow, so shall you reap, I say to them all.

In fact, looking back, I can't remember a time when I felt like a 'member of society' – my old man and my mother and everyone else of their generation saw to that. They blew it.

And the result was me, and thousands more like me, alienated and discontent. With chips on our fucking shoulders, if you like.

Well, fuck Nicole too, I thought.

So I bought some chips, got on the train without a ticket and went to a place I called home.

'Why don't you get it trimmed up a bit, just round here, and take these bits off here? Can't you brush it over like everyone does? You'd look much nicer.' Mother touched my hair at the back and sides, then looked me up and down but decided against saying anything about my clothes.

'Leave off, will you. What's for tea?'

'Liver. Your father would be much happier.' She began taking things out of the cupboards ready for the evening cooking ritual.

She was quite shapely as far as mums went, with nice tits, and good-looking too. I knew my mates would have liked to shag her because I in turn fancied their mums and visualised them during masturbation, usually sucking me off.

I wondered then what it would be like to shag my own mother. To be sucked off by my own mother. A terrible unspoken thing. Am I depraved? I suppose so, but then everyone I know is if that's the case. Rolfe used to watch his mum through the lavatory keyhole, then tell us all about it in class. But Goggles used to shag his dog – that has to be more depraved.

Or is it?

At school they taught me that according to ancient Greeks, mother-shagging's all right. And smart people discuss it at depth, debating all the different aspects to it. But if it's someone from a council estate doing the business, it's disgusting.

There we go, class again.

As I see it, the only real problem is babies being born with two heads and stuff like that, the 'genetic problem', as our biology teacher put it. Apparently, related white rats which shag together eventually produce non-standard offspring. I mean, not because they're depraved – I don't know whether you can get depraved rats – but because their genetic characteristics become exaggerated.

But how do we know we're not already warped beyond recognition as a so-called human race anyway? Does anyone really know what a human being is supposed to look like? Maybe if our ancestors hadn't been so 'depraved', the human race would look entirely different today.

'What are you thinking about?' asked mother suddenly. Mums read minds.

'Nothing.'

Then she came across all pleading. 'Go and have just a little trim up before your father comes home – I'll give you the money. Why don't you get them to blow wave it? Why you have to have it sticking up all over the show like that I do not know.'

'Why don't you give it a break? I'm not at bleeding school any more.' I didn't dare say 'fucking'; there'd be murders.

Change of attack. 'No. And it's about time you got yourself a decent job, instead of all this casual work you've been doing.'

I'd explained the new clothes away by saying I was doing casual work in factories. The only trouble was I had to get up in the morning to look as if I was going out to work, then creep back later and hope that none of the neighbours would say anything.

'And all this staying out all night at friends' houses – I don't believe you.' She fixed me with her stare, the 'look me straight in the eye' number, which I'd learned to fake like a master through years of lying to adults.

I stared back unflinching. 'Believe what you like. If I want to go out, I'll go out.'

'Well that's what you think! If you think you can walk in and out of this house just as it pleases you, you've got another think coming!'

This was the way it always was, emotional. Nothing could be discussed reasonably without someone flying off the handle.

'Why can't I?'

'Don't you get tricky with me!' Her voice was threatening now. 'You can't because I say so. And your father says so. Now mind out of the way.' She pushed me aside to throw potatoes into the sink. Beneath the table the dog was shaking in little spasms and looking anywhere but at us. He was no fool.

I should have stood by my principles, said 'Forget it' and walked out there and then, but I was hungry, so I went into the living-room and switched on the television. I couldn't hear it because of her scraping the potatoes viciously and throwing her weight around, so I turned it up and sat down just as the old man's key sounded in the door.

He walked in. 'You bloody deaf or something? Turn that down,' he said in greeting, pleased to see his son.

I got up and adjusted the volume while he took off his mac. He always wore his gabardine mac.

He next went into the kitchen, asked my mother if she was all right and kicked off his shoes. Then he put on his leather indoor slippers, came back into the living-room rustling his *Evening News* into shape and sat down in his chair. It would be but a short space of time before he started, I knew that. You could always tell by his moods, and his worst ones were fearsome. Still.

Even now he scared me, although the hidings had long stopped.

He started. 'Have you got yourself a job yet?' he asked, as if interviewing someone. Despite coming from a very poor background, he had cultivated an 'educated' accent to get on in life.

'I've been doing some casual work and there's more of that if I want it.'

He lowered his paper and looked at me. 'I said, "Have you got yourself a job yet?"'

I looked confused, although I knew what he meant. 'What do you mean?' I asked, trying to sound as if I cared.

'What I mean is,' he leaned forward, 'have – you – got – your – self – a – job – yet? Or is that too much to ask of that bloody thick head of yours? A JOB. A proper job that you get up to go to five or six days a week, which pays you a proper wage, which you then bring home and share with your mother to help pay for your keep. Do you understand that? Work and pay, it's called.'

'Well, no . . .'

'Are you doing anything about it?'

A few years ago I would have started crying in the hope that my mother would intervene, but I was too old for that now and imagined that my friends could see me. In my mind I compared the two lives I was leading, and felt like a fraud. Sooner or later I would have to choose between them. 'There's nothing I've seen that I really fancy,' I whined, knowing that whatever I said would be the wrong thing. After all, the last thing he wanted to hear was anything which could be seen as being remotely successful on my part. His sole objective was to convince my mother what a cunt I was. Making me feel the same way was a little bonus, but I wasn't falling for that any more.

'Nothing that you really *fancy*?' he mocked spitefully. 'Just who do you think you are?' He was sneering now. 'Three fucking GCEs and you can't find anything you *fancy*?' He laughed bitterly. 'I've seen men with university degrees sweep the streets, and thankful for the chance to contribute something, but all you do is take, like most of your poxy generation. You make me shit. And while we're on the subject of shit, do something about your appearance before I do.' He glared, then raised his paper, expelling air with an audible 'pfffff' from between his pursed lips.

There was the sharp tapping of metal on china from the kitchen as dinner was dished up and the three of us sat down around the table and ate silently. Afterwards, I went upstairs and listened with some satisfaction to my parents' raised voices as they argued about me while I washed and changed. Then, without asking, I took money from my mother's purse and went out.

The thing was, I reasoned, I couldn't please them both without losing my identity. And I'd never please my father anyway because he was competing with me for my mother's affection. You know, most people just don't realise how dangerous it is having children; I mean, who in their right mind would dream of inviting a complete stranger to share their home for the foreseeable future? As much as I hate it, I can understand why parents try to mould their kids into something. It's through fear.

Striding up the hill towards the station, I vowed to end the struggle by emptying my heart of any feeling I felt towards them. Only in that way, I reasoned, could I become free. I owed it to myself.

With these noble thoughts coursing through my brain, I arrived at the station to find Sue Glover waiting there for her date, who hadn't turned up. She was an attractive blonde girl who tended to keep herself to herself and for the life of me I couldn't understand why anyone would want to stand her up; she dressed as stylishly as any girl I knew and even had that peculiarly fashionable elbows-back-chin-forward way of walking that some boys and girls were beginning to adopt, but perhaps part of the attraction was that she kept out of the mainstream and nobody knew much about her.

On impulse, I asked if she fancied coming up the West End. She looked at her watch. 'Yeah, why not? If he can't be bothered to turn up on time, that's his problem.' Then she put her arm in mine, smiled and waited to be whisked away.

Well. Here was the girl whom everyone lusted after hanging on to my arm, clip-clopping along beside me in her calf-length black pin-stripe skirt, sheer white blouse with a long collar and three-quarter-length blue suede coat as we walked down the stairs and on to the platform. A train came in within seconds and we stepped aboard and found a seat, and I was pleased to note that she didn't eye up any of the other geezers who got on and off. This one had real class, a real sweetie.

'Where we going then?' she asked.

I didn't want to risk taking her to La Discothèque or the Flamingo in case Sherri was there, so I suggested the Scene round the back of Windmill Street.

'What time does it shut?' she asked.

'Four.'

'Then what?'

'Have you got to get home?'

'No. It's just all that hanging about until the first train I don't like.'

'The last train's at 12.25. Or we could kip in a siding.'

She didn't like the idea of that. 'A friend of mine said that you could get into the Regent Palace Hotel without paying. All you have to do is walk in and find an empty room.'

'We'll do that then.' I grinned at her, amazed at the pace of things but trying not to look too keen.

She smiled back. 'An empty room with two beds,' she added, 'one for you and one for me.'

But did she really mean it?

I thought about the evening: the promise of sex, the forty-three purple hearts I had in my pocket, the Scene, and wondered how to squeeze them all in. If she was a prick-teaser like someone had said, it wouldn't matter whether I did the speed or not. If she wasn't a prick-teaser it would be a shame to find out when I was speeding out of my brains. On the other hand, I wanted to do the speed whatever happened, so the sex had to come first. The problem was how to get round to the subject after just fifteen minutes. Okay, we'd seen each other about a few times and said 'hello', and I'd been out with a couple of her mates, but we weren't exactly close friends.

I thought about it: I'd have to trick her. Maybe we could come in from the Regent Street side and approach the Scene from that angle, so that we had to walk right past the Regent Palace. All I had to do then was suggest we try out how easy it was to get in first, because then we could relax for the rest of the evening knowing one way or the other whether we could stay or whether we had to catch the last train. With this plan in mind I led her across Trafalgar Square and up Haymarket towards Piccadilly, then continued on up Regent Street instead of Windmill Street.

It was easier than I thought. Arm in arm and looking confident, we walked through the foyer and up the stairs without being challenged. On the first floor we found three rooms unlocked and unoccupied, chose one and went in. Inside, everything was brown and beige and worn, but the bed was too prominent to be ignored, so I casually asked her what she wanted to do. I wasn't sure myself. Faced with the room, the bed, the privacy, the seemingly unlimited time and the pretty girl, I wasn't sure where to begin, and, if I was really, really honest, I'd never done it properly before.

'What do you mean "what do I want to do"?' she asked with her nose slightly in the air, as if picking up a whiff of deception.

'Well, do you want to stay here for a while?'

'What for?' She sat on the edge of the bed and bounced up and down. Could I handle this?

Sitting down next to her, I put my arm around her shoulder and pulled her to me. Then we kissed, violently, open-mouthed, and she spat a big globule of saliva into my mouth. Trying not to appear disgusted – she had done it so naturally that I assumed it was something some people did – I managed to pass the saliva back without appearing like I was rejecting her. She then passed it back and seemed to be getting worked up about it, panting and dribbling and pulling off her coat, all the time keeping her eyes shut tight. With one eye slightly open I found her blouse buttons and slipped a hand around her tit. Gasping, she pulled open my fly and began rubbing my dick so furiously it was painful.

'Hang on! Hang on!' I hissed, and pushed her back on to the bed. I thought of her mum and dad just then, sitting somewhere, probably watching *Take Your Pick* with Michael Miles, unaware that their daughter was holding my cock and was about to be fucked. I pushed her skirt up high.

'Out of bounds,' she gasped, eyes still shut.

I ignored what she said and tried to put my hand inside her knickers.

She opened her eyes as she pulled my hand away. 'You can't,' she said, more firmly this time.

'Why not?'

She hesitated. Here it comes, I thought; she's on. So what? I could put up with that.

'It's sewn up,' she said.

'Sewn up? What do you mean it's sewn up?'

'They said it had to be sewn up because I was too . . . promiscuous.'

I'd never heard that one before. And it never occurred to me that she might not be telling the truth; even at seventeen I still wasn't really aware of the fundamentals of the human body. Confused, I suggested we go on to the Scene, and while she reapplied her make-up, I swallowed thirty hearts and quietly left her to sort her life out.

* * *

'. . . Just because you've become a young man now, my momma told me, you'd better shop around, oh yeah, you'd better shop around . . .'

Yeah, Smokey, nice . . .

Down Brewer Street towards Walkers Court, fuck the Scene, never did like it there – too many trendies and up-and-coming pop stars putting themselves about with their flash middle-class tarts. These are the ones who steal our ideas and get paid for it. I don't mind that but they get it all wrong, miss the point, the style that you only understand when you're there, living it. And these geezers are too precious for that. I don't blame the girls because they see money as power and want to produce strong babies and guarantee the survival of the species and all that stuff. And if you're a geezer with stacks of dosh you can look rich and fuck about and generally have a savage time pulling the women knowing that if it all goes wrong someone's going to bail you out because you're valuable. Not like us, who have to survive knowing that as soon as you fart in the wrong direction some official cunt just waiting for the chance to inflict damage is going to be on you.

Who you fucking looking at? Yeah, go on, fuck off. Can't stand these cunts who give you the eyeball.

Wardour Street again. Wonder what Sue's doing. Probably checking her stitches. Huh! Maybe I should borrow Greeny's razor – he's got a cut-throat razor which he uses to stripe people who upset him, right fucking nutter he is, and I admire him for damaging people like that because it makes people think twice before they fuck about with our lot. I'm going to get one. They reckon a nice neat stripe with a razor leaves a bigger scar because the meat slips about instead of being able to key into something. Thinking about it, I wouldn't mind a nice little scar myself, on the side of my cheek, slanted, about an inch and a half long, just below my left eye.

Nice girl in a strip-club booth winks at me. Ginger the queer's on the other side of the street, a good geezer. Ging, how you going? Oh, all right, love, but it's bloody dead tonight – what you doing? Don't know, just wandering, probably go down La Discothèque. Might see you later; bye, love. Now that's funny – he's queer but he don't bother me at all. One of the crowd, I suppose. There's queers and there's queers, know what I mean? You often see him pulling drunks.

Up Shaftesbury Avenue towards Cambridge Circus, timeless traffic and people everywhere, but I'm just observing, hungry, predatory, looking for excitement of any kind; lots of bumpkins disguising theirselves as Beatles with long-fringe hairdos and jackets without lapels, and flares or drainpipes, really rate theirselves, cunts. They attract the girls from the sticks who haven't got a clue, who buy Kiss-Me-Quick hats and tins of London fog and fray the bottoms of their jeans and wear striped blue-and-white matelot shirts and tan moccasins and have big lacquered hair. Stuff that was happening ages ago.

Being Modernist is supposed to be where it's at, but I don't go for this labelling stuff because I'm a smart geezer. What it's all about is wearing something exclusive, something not in the wrong colour. Everyone wants to know what the right colour is, but it's not the right colour that's important, it's the wrong colour.

Then you've got to front it and at the same time be part of the scene. Nice strides, where did you get them? Like your shirt, where did you get it? Nice shoes, how much did you pay for them? Nylon macs, not only blue but brown, and maroon, and green. I've got a *light* green one and these cunts wouldn't even know where to find a blue one even if they realised they existed. And these pink cotton strides – smart, but they're finished – John Michael's got a pair in the window now. Nice three-inch gap between them and my Toppers loafers.

Fucking Beatle boots. It was them that copied the Mod fashion. Handmade Anello and Davide two-tones were all right and the Cuban heels make you taller but they've been done to death. As soon as the fashion experts grab the idea it's dead. Look at all these gawking day-trippers. Need rolling, the whole fucking lot of them.

Need a friendly face bad, wanna talk like mad.

And who do I see across the road? Recognise his gaunt face with the thin curved nose anywhere. It's Frankie with Norma gassing to some old geezer. Norma walks off with him. Skip through the traffic. Frankie, how you going? He's bleached his light-brown hair.

'All right.' He eyes me up and down, checking my gear. 'What you up to?'

'Looking.'

'I'll come with you. Got any pills?'

'No, only about a dozen.'

Cut down into Gerrard Street and back towards La Discothèque, where there's a crowd standing outside.

'Where you going for the bank holiday – Clacton?' he asks.

'There or Brighton. Probably Brighton. There's supposed to be a party there. Someone Mac knows.'

'D'you hear any more about that geezer down the caves, the one you were fighting with?'

'Kenser Donnelly. No, he's all right. Someone saw him up the Fifty-Nine Club, as lairy as usual.'

'I'll give him lairy if I see him again. If he's down the coast we'll have the cunt.' He adjusts his pink gingham tab collar and sticks his jaw out to free his neck skin. 'Here comes Ringo Starr,' he says, staring ahead at an approaching lone male, another Beatle devotee. 'Let's see how he's fixed.'

As we come face to face, Beatle boy tries to pass.

'Hold it, hold it,' says Frankie, looking evil again. 'What's the fucking hurry?'

'Sorry, mate, I was just trying to get by.' Ringo is already scared and shouldn't be out on his own.

'Got any money?' asks Frankie.

He hesitates and gives the game away. 'No.'

'Don't be silly,' I say. 'Just hand the money over otherwise you're going to get a spank, right?' I'm worried that Frankie might start getting ideas about using his knife again, and I want to go to La Discothèque to see if Sherri's there, preferably without being covered in blood. Apart from which, the last thing I need right now is a fifteen-year stretch.

Beatle boy looks desperately about, but Frankie grabs him by the shirt collar before he can shout for help. Between us we relieve him of just over six pounds and ten purple hearts and send him on his way with a warning not to squeal.

* * *

After dividing the loot, Frankie went to look for Norma and I went on to the club, but Sherri wasn't there so I relegated her to the distant boundaries of my mind. Probably never see her again. Neither was Mac – he was out with a bird somewhere – nor Dinger, who was at a family wedding, so I ended up talking all night to Sheila, a sort from Hackney with a nice pair of bristols.

At three, she went home with her friend and I drifted back towards Leicester Square and bumped into Freddy Newman, an old school friend, who'd just arrived after hitching from his girlfriend's place in Bromley. Like me, he was at a loose end, so we walked down to the Embankment to see if anyone was hanging out there.

Just by St Martin's in the Fields, a large white Cadillac pulled up alongside us. Inside were two males, the driver about twenty-five, light-brown hair, trendy, the passenger older, black hair, thick sideburns, swarthy – a right dodgy-looking character.

But the driver spoke in a soft, well-educated way. 'Where are you lads going? Can we give you a lift anywhere?'

'The Embankment, if you like,' I said. I didn't consider for a moment the possibilities or the reasons why two older males should be trying to pick up two younger males at half past three in the morning. I was still far too naïve for that, despite Greek Toni.

'Do you want to come to a party?' he asked.

What! A stroke of luck or what . . .

We leapt in the back of the car and spread ourselves out over the big white leather seats, exchanging glances of disbelief. Neither of the two men spoke as we glided smoothly towards Knightsbridge, and we just sat staring out of the windows at the empty streets, hoping that some-one we knew would see us being chauffeured about in a big white Cadillac.

A few minutes later, we pulled up inside a courtyard of terraced mews houses and stepped out into the cool night air, but there was no sign of a party anywhere. We followed the men up some stairs and into an old coach house.

'Come in, boys,' said the older man. 'What's your names?'

'I'm Tom and he's Frederick.'

'Freddy.'

He showed us to a couple of flash white settees in an alcove and asked if we'd like a drink, so I went for a Bacardi and Coke with ice and lemon and Freddy a Scotch and dry ginger with ice, and I was still wondering when the party was going to start when the younger bloke – Andrew, he called himself – brought back two full tumblers and the bottles.

'Here. Don't be afraid to help yourself,' he said pleasantly. 'There's plenty more.'

The other one introduced himself as Lionel and began to question us about our lives, and slowly it dawned on me that the party was going to be just the four of us. Nice.

These very nice guys wanted to shag *us*. At least, that's how it looked to me. A homosexual approach for the second time in a few weeks. First Toni, now Lionel and Andrew. The names weren't out of place, anyway. Hello Toni, hello Andrew, hello Lionel. Three nice boys. But I was going to have to knock wearing all this pink gear on the head and get back to the traditional blue-for-a-boy stuff.

No, fuck that. I'd end up looking like everyone else.

God appeared keen to show me what it was like to be a girl, an object of male desire, and I didn't like it too much, flattering though it was. Maybe the lesson was that I should try and be nicer to girls in future, stop making them feel that the only reason I was going out with them was for sex. But that *was* the only reason.

The snag was there wasn't much chance of being able to fight my way out of this one because both of them were bigger than me. In fact Lionel was like a gorilla. And Freddy didn't have a clue about fighting; he was more like a girl.

More like a girl. That's it! I always thought there was something funny about him.

Fuck, this Bacardi's a bit strong.

More like a girl, eh? It all fits now.

I glanced at him and he seemed to be enjoying himself, smiling and being friendly, sipping his drink.

Was he queer?

Shit.

All this time and Freddy's a queer.

Surely not.

He pulls some tasty birds. He's got a girlfriend; I've seen her, and very nice too. Too good for him, in fact.

On the other hand, he never lasts long with them; a few days and they're off.

The alcohol was reviving the speed now, giving me a

little confidence booster and counteracting its own effects so that I wasn't getting pissed, but Freddy hadn't done any pills (he didn't agree with drugs, he said) and was getting giggly and throwing his hands all over the place. Just like a girl.

Soon Lionel was concentrating on him, being all understanding and attentive and constantly topping up his glass, while Andrew took it upon himself to show me around the house. It was all right in a poncey way but everything seemed to be white or with strong sexual overtones: pictures of naked people, pink curtains and drapes, statues of naked men wrestling and holding each other's dicks . . . and I started to toy with the idea of braining Andrew with one of them and making a dash for it while I still had the chance. What if they'd drugged the drinks? Thinking about it made my head swim.

'Don't look so aggressive,' he said, smiling.

'You're queers, aren't you?' I growled.

He laughed. 'Not particularly. I'm not going to rape you, if that's what you're worried about.'

'I know you're fucking not.' I tried to look hard.

At that moment Lionel swept in looking pleased with himself and announced that he was tired and wanted to go to bed. 'Can you sort out a bed for Tommy?' he asked Andrew, then left the room.

Looks like he was shacking up with Freddy.

I looked menacingly at Andrew. 'Now what?' I asked.

'You can share my bed.'

'Fuck off.'

He laughed aloud. He was all right, actually; I just didn't fancy someone reaming my arsehole. 'I told you, I won't touch you,' he insisted. 'Look, I'll put pillows down the middle of the bed.' He started to arrange the bed into two distinct halves. When he'd finished, he undressed and got in. Seconds later he was snoring. Quietly I removed my shoes and climbed carefully into the other side, where I lay wide awake and wired up, staring at the ceiling as the speed euphoria disintegrated into another comedown.

Whether Freddy was queer or not I never found out – he may have wondered the same about me – but he refused to talk about it the next day or ever again, except to say that Lionel and Andrew were in showbusiness, so I assumed the worst and blew him out. If he'd said yes, I wouldn't have minded so much, but as far as I was concerned there were no secrets among friends. You want to keep secrets, then fuck off. Lionel and Andrew – who the fuck were they anyway? I'd never heard of them.

A week later, Sue Glover caught up with me. Walking towards my parents' house, deep in thought about where I was going to get some money from and whether I would at last have to go and find a job, I heard a breathless female voice shout out my name. Turning, I saw her running down the hill after me, as beautiful as usual, her tits dancing in front of her.

'Tommy! Tommy!' She stared as if searching for something in my face. 'I'm . . . sorry . . . about last weekend.'

Relief flooded through me; I had imagined she was going to accuse me of something terrible, like abandoning her. My ingrained guilt complex coming out, I suppose.

Laughing casually, I said, 'Don't worry about it.'

'You haven't told anyone, have you?'

'About what?'

'What I said . . . the stitches and all that.'

'Why should I do that?'

'It's just . . . well, it's not true.'

Aha! The crafty cow has a novel way of keeping randy boys at bay.

'I didn't think it was, but I couldn't see the point of

making anything of it,' I said casually, pretending to look at something more interesting across the road. Makes you feel good, having people grovel before you, especially when you don't deserve it.

She looked awkward, and the thought crossed my mind to take her home and try again while her defences were down, but it would depend on the time – mother got home at five. 'What's the time?' I asked.

She looked at her watch. 'Quarter past five. Look, I'm sorry if I'm holding you up, but I wanted to ask you if you fancied coming to a party tomorrow night at Sandy Dean's house.'

Fuck. Quarter past five. Too late by about half an hour. 'Who's going?' I asked absent-mindedly.

'A few of Sandy's friends from work and some others from the estate. Her mum and dad's going out and they said she could have a few friends round. I just thought you might like to come. I could meet you there or outside the station again.'

'All right, I'll see you there,' I said, walking away. 'Remember to take your stitches out first.' Sometimes I was so flash I made myself cringe.

Next morning I met Dinger and we jumped on a train to the West End. Big brother Vince was all he talked about: how he was doing really well, how smart he was, how he looked after mother and the old man, how he had hospitalised sister Brenda's husband for knocking her about. How he had forked out four grand to help out an uncle who was setting up in business. Vince was a big man and not to be crossed, he said. 'He's got a shooter, an automatic. I've seen it. Keeps it in his wardrobe. And you should see the knife he's got – I saw it one day covered in blood.'

No doubt Dinger was exaggerating as usual. But when you live in crowded places, you can't help hearing rumours.

'Ask him if he can get me some work. Something like you do,' I said.

Dinger had described how he was a sort of office boy to Vince, running errands for him on a daily cash-in-hand basis. Apparently he had other businesses apart from the fruit stall, which Dinger said was only a front anyway.

'I'll ask him, but I doubt if he'll have anything – he keeps trying to find *me* a proper job; says he don't want me mixing with the people he knows.'

Not a lot of chance there then. Not that I really wanted to work for anyone. I just wanted to get my old man off my back. All the time he's going on about work, work, work. So's my mother. I gave up pretending about casual work so that I could lie in bed longer in the mornings, and it's made them ten times worse. I tell you, you're better off lying. They just want me out of the house during the day so that I can't bring the dollies back. I got Jill Callaghan back the other day but had to rush her out through the back door when the old man came home early. I couldn't believe it. It had taken me two hours of hard work getting it across to her how smooth I was, plying her with vodka from the drinks cupboard, so that she would let me get her tits out, when suddenly I saw him walk past the front window. I shoved her out of the back door so hard she fell over and grazed her knees; really blew it.

To tell you the truth, they're both getting seriously on my nerves – him with his moods and long, threatening silences and glares, and her with the constant nagging about money, clothes, hairstyles, the way I talk, the fucking lot. The worst thing was when I forgot about the bits of screwed-up bog roll I'd left under the bed after wanking, and she'd cleaned the room. I'd used a sock as well. She acted strange and offhand for a week and I wondered why until suddenly I had a hot flush and remembered that I'd forgotten to clear up. So what? Bollocks. The secret's out. Big deal.

At Charing Cross we got off the train and walked out into the sunshine, the West End like a breath of fresh air. Familiar smells of coffee and drains and petrol fumes.

'We should find ourselves a couple of birds and put them on the game like Frankie,' said Dinger suddenly. 'Don't you know anyone who'd do it?'

I thought about it: Norma did it for Frankie because she was crazy about him. She'd eat his shit if he told her to. Finding a sort like that would be difficult, and anyway, I couldn't do it. I respected girls too much, believe it or not.

But there was another way. 'All we need is someone who's up for a bit of fun,' I replied.

'Well, I know that . . .' Dinger looked at me as if I was daft.

'No . . . I mean, no shagging, just a laugh – a few threats and a quick getaway.'

'What are you talking about?'

'I was talking to a sortie from Hackney in La Discothèque last week. I know she'd do it. She said she'd be in the Coffee Anne this morning. All we've got to do is get her to pull some old geezer, take him back somewhere, and roll him.'

Dinger liked that.

Accelerating across Trafalgar Square towards the basement café, we scattered the pigeons as we went just to annoy the day-trippers up from the sticks who didn't have to live with the pigeon shit. And, sure enough, Sheila was there with her frothy coffee and a Raoul's shoe bag.

After the usual stuff, introducing Dinger and all that, I went straight into it and asked if she wanted to earn some money. I was right, she was all for it. 'I haven't got to do anything,' she asked, 'just get them in there and you do the rest?'

'Exactly that,' I said.

After finishing our coffee we set out for Brewer Street. The plan was that she would pull the richest-looking and oldest man she could find and take him straight to the Regent Palace Hotel, where we would already have opened the side door for her. She was to go to the first floor, where we would be waiting.

It went without a hitch, exactly according to plan. Sheila was a natural. Within minutes of us installing ourselves in a shady alcove on the first floor she arrived with a punter, an old bloke with yellow hair and a Crombie overcoat. As instructed she found an empty room and we watched the door close softly behind them.

'Let's wait a bit for a laugh,' I suggested. 'See how far he gets with her.'

But Dinger was on one of his honourable numbers. 'Don't be a cunt. She's all right,' he said. 'Anyway, if she gets scared off now, she won't do it again, will she?' He had a point.

Suddenly there was a scream and a crash and the door was flung open. Sheila burst out looking mad. 'Dirty old bastard!' she screamed, storming off down the corridor.

I ran and grabbed her by the arm. 'Hang on! Hang on! Wait here.'

Inside, the old man was sitting on the bed nursing his head. All around lay pieces of what looked like a vase.

'Okay,' I said to him, 'what's going on? Are you hurting my little sister, you fucking pervert?'

Startled, he looked up and groaned. 'All right, all right, what do you want?'

'Compensation,' said Dinger. He'd heard Vince talk of 'compensation'.

'Compensation, you bloody little thugs? Listen, I'm not so green as you may think, so fuck off before I call the police.'

This was unexpected. The trouble was, we were giving him time to think and talk back. I called out for Sheila. Warily she peered round the door, then came back in.

'Sister,' I said, 'tell us what he did.'

She glared at the old man. 'He wanted me to suck him off, the filthy old bastard.'

At this he jumped up and tried to reach the door, but we wrestled him on to the floor and found his wallet while he lay struggling feebly beneath us. Quickly we removed the notes, put the wallet back in his pocket and left after threatening him to stay quiet.

He was loaded. We made forty pounds each for thirty minutes' work. Two weeks' wages. And Sheila was already planning the next one. Now we could pay for a room in a hotel and she could take the punters back without worrying about getting involved with the hotel staff. Once in the room she'd make sure they got their trousers down and we'd come in. Simple. Apart from that, all she had to do was make sure they were weak and had a few quid on them.

And it worked. By mid-afternoon we'd made enough money to call it a day. We were all jubilant, and Sheila asked if I fancied going back to Hackney with her, but it would have created problems for the rest of the day. I had things to buy.

On the train back, Dinger asked why I hadn't gone to Hackney. 'You know you could have shagged that,' he said.

To tell you the truth, the thought hadn't occurred to me – I was too busy thinking about money.

That night I went to Sandy Dean's party wearing clothes

that cost close on a hundred pounds. In my pockets I carried another fifty quid and enough speed to take everyone through the roof.

Sue was all over me from the beginning but being already blocked I had no choice but to fend her off and she took it personally, accusing me sulkily of using her and inviting gatecrashers – Mac and Dinger and a couple of others – to the already over-full house. And Sandy Dean was panicking. 'If Mummy and Daddy come home and see this lot here they'll go mad,' she cried. It was a nice neat house with fancy furniture and fitted carpets and murals of mountain scenes and little gold chandeliers I'd seen for sale on the stalls in East Lane.

Things were lively but safe, as far as I could make out – the only naughtiness being that Mummy and Daddy's drink, including a prized collection of miniatures from all around the world, had been drunk within an hour of the party starting – but the atmosphere changed badly when a little gang of local motorbike boys, friends of someone in the family, arrived. The problem was that one of them, Malcolm, a sort of ginger James Dean with studs, was drunk, and his one-time girlfriend was Sue, who was clinging on to me again, frightened that he might get aggressive.

'He's really nasty when he gets upset – he nearly killed someone in Battersea Park last year,' she said suddenly. He'd also received a kicking down Chislehurst Caves. Nothing to do with me.

Oh yeah. As much as I liked this exhibition of confidence in my ability to cope with the animal – who, according to some stirrer, was now looking for Sue – I felt that I was being set up. I mean, I hadn't touched the bird. It would have been different if I'd been giving her one behind his back, but I'd only met her to talk to last weekend. Anyway, they'd split up nearly two years ago.

We were standing in the kitchen, leaning up against the fridge, hidden behind a crush of bodies.

'Let's go to the bedroom,' I said, hoping that he might go away if he couldn't find her – forgetting that if he did find her in the bedroom with me he might get even more upset.

Easing our way through the crowd into the hallway, we could see Malcolm standing in the living-room with his pals, guzzling beer from a bottle like it was the last beer left in the world. Sue pulled aside Sandy, who, having drunk too much, had suddenly given up worrying about her parents and was groping on the stairs with a bloke from Deptford. 'If anyone asks,' said Sue, 'tell them I've gone home, okay?'

Bedroom one was full. As was bedroom two. But bedroom three only had three couples in it, and we found a space on the carpet between the bed and the far wall to lie down together; it was probably the safest place in the house.

Sue's lips were searching for mine in the darkness and she took my hand and placed it at the top of her legs. Our tongues snaked about and she became breathless again, but she didn't spit in my mouth this time. And it was a real shame that I was blocked. 'Finger me, finger me,' she moaned aloud, which got everyone giggling, and she started massaging my crotch but suddenly pulled back when she realised I wasn't getting a hard on. 'Don't you fancy me?' she whispered.

I very quietly explained the effects of speed. Having been out with Malcolm, the only speed she knew about was on the back of his bike. And I thought she was a Mod.

'How long does it take to wear off?' she asked.

'A few hours.'

'Oh, great. I'll just go and put the kettle on then.'

Before I could laugh, the door burst open and there he stood, mad Malcolm, silhouetted against the hallway light, clutching an empty beer bottle, groping for the light switch, but someone had taken the bulb out. Cursing, he peered into the gloom. 'Sue, you in there?' he shouted. She tensed up next to me as I peered cautiously over the bed, but as luck would have it he saw me.

'You! Oi you!' he shouted as I tried to duck out of sight. 'I want to talk to you. Who's that with you? Have you got my bird there?'

'I'm not your bird,' screeched Sue.

Picking up an empty vodka bottle from the floor, I slowly stood up. Rearranging her clothes, Sue stood up behind me, and for a moment we all stood just looking at each other. Then a bottle flew through the air and smashed on the wall by his head as someone in the room took offence at his attitude, and in reply he hurled the beer bottle in our direction but missed, smashing it instead against the wall behind. I aimed the vodka bottle at his head, but as he ducked it flew through the doorway and down into the stairwell, smashing somewhere below. Then a wine bottle from someone else struck him a glancing blow on the temple and he retreated quickly back down the stairs. Like lightning we were after him, encouraged by the effects of our combined efforts, but a riot had by now erupted below, and mad, systematic wrecking began. The television was thrown through the front window; every bottle in the house, including those full of milk, was thrown and smashed against walls, floors and ceilings; doors were ripped from their hinges and thrown through closed windows; chairs were smashed and trampled to firewood; and Malcolm, after jabbing a glass in Mac's face, was finally cornered in the kitchen and stabbed in the neck with a broken light-ale bottle. A fountain of blood sprayed over everyone around, up the walls and on to the ceiling, and Sandy, who'd been running around the house screaming hysterically, fainted.

As we were leaving, trying to sponge the blood from our clothes with wet tea-towels, two ambulances arrived, followed almost immediately by Sandy's mum and dad, who just stood and stared with their mouths open at what was left of the house. All around, the neighbours stood and watched, doing nothing to help. No police arrived and nobody was reported. That's the way it was. A week later Sandy was out dancing, laughing about it; she'd come up in the world, having transcended her former image by wrecking her parents' house.

Brighton that August bank holiday was quiet. Dinger and Mac – whose facial injuries were nothing (in fact, they made him better-looking) – stayed with two local girls they'd met at the party we'd gone down there for, a boring event made even worse by the non-stop playing of Beatles and Dave Clark Five records, while I decided to hitch to Hastings to see what was happening there. Outside Palace Pier I met a kid from Lewisham I knew from the West End, Johnny W, who was as bored as I was, and we set out together, hoping to find some action.

Arriving in Hastings just before midnight on Sunday, we found the place deserted and cold. Everything was shut. We tried the nick to see if they'd put us up for the night, but they told us to fuck off and sleep on the beach, which we did, under a pile of deck-chairs, and froze.

Dawn the next day saw us hitching back to Brighton, cold, hungry and dejected, and by the time we got there the holiday was over, the trippers gone and the seafront deserted except for the usual drab crowd and a couple of gangs of bikers strutting about eating fish and chips and throwing the paper everywhere. Pissed off, we jumped a train back to London, went to the Roaring Twenties in Carnaby Street, a black ska club, and smoked some weed for the first time, but it didn't work.

After August, the winter seemed to close in around us and descend into darkness. Magazines frequently referred to us now as 'Mods' and issued guidelines as to how to look and behave. Thousands of kids, realising a trend was in the offing, began to creep out of the woodwork wearing desert boots, Hush Puppies, Fred Perry shirts and white socks, which nobody who had a scrap of self-esteem would have worn. They invaded the West End clubs and in the process destroyed the exclusive atmosphere which until then had been the main attraction.

Most of these kids, clueless and devoid of imagination, flair and style, imitated the fakes they saw on *Ready, Steady, Go*, a crap television show hosted by an out-of-place, middle-aged, middle-class prick that promoted, with one or two exceptions, everything we rejected. They tried telling us what we were, how we lived, where we went, what we wore, how we danced, everything, invading the space we'd found for ourselves, so that we had to work hard to avoid being tarred with the same brush as the fakes.

Then The Who began to promote themselves as Mod icons, and we knew it was time to move on.

One very cold night, a group of us met almost by chance in a pub out of town in Bromley before going on to Bromley Court Hotel, where Sonny Boy Williamson or Muddy Waters or John Lee Hooker or Inez and Charlie Foxx was playing – I can't remember who it was – and we decided spontaneously on a course of action. Barely a thing needed to be said; we'd each of us been persecuted from birth by other people trying to tell us how to live and hurting us when we refused to conform, but now we had the Commercial Squad on our tail like bloodhounds, destroying everything we'd created.

Some arsehole had earned a buck or two by stating in a magazine that youngsters like us, or 'Mods', were gentle, middle-class boys who fancied themselves as artists and trendsetters, tending to form in male groups and sometimes wearing make-up. All the stylistic creation, the clothes, the music, was a middle-class thing, apparently.

It might have been funny had it not been such an obvious two-fingered attempt at what the fashion world was very good at, namely stealing working-class ideas, and as the article was read aloud we could all see that extreme measures were going to be needed to force them to eat their fucking words.

Easter 1964. Cold and grey. The word was Clacton. Some went and some didn't. I didn't because I went to Brighton.

In Clacton the non-biker kids finally became known worldwide as 'Mods' – despite the many and varied articles of dress they wore – and the motorbike boys and girls became known as 'Rockers'. Then they all got bored having nothing to do, gathered in unusually large groups only to be insulted by the locals, and finally, urged on by Frankie and a couple of others, went around town being unpleasant to anyone who asked for it. And a few that didn't.

Then all the world realised what a boring shit-hole Clacton really was and it died forever.

Brighton, on the other hand, despite being cold and grey, was welcoming. Its daughters took us in and shagged us, fed and watered us, took us out and showed us off, and did it all over again. There was little trouble to talk of and the Brighton police were proud of their ability to keep things in order. But they didn't know that we'd already underlined the town, along with Margate, for the next bank holiday, Whitsun, when, with a bit of luck, the weather would be a bit better.

Clacton was a trial run, just to test the reaction, to see the sort of resistance we might come up against, and in the main it was only the Essex and east London crowd that wanted to go. But the papers made a meal of it, and managed to get it all wrong.

According to one paper, 'a tearaway called "Red" roared into town' on a 'supercharged' scooter. He wore a black jacket and carried a bird on the pillion wearing 'shades' and thigh-length boots. Some Mods. The hilarious thing was that he was supposed to be screaming, 'Fun, fun, fun!' Can you imagine it? On a *supercharged* scooter?

There was 'an orgy of destruction', and Clacton folk were afraid for their lives, preferring to stay indoors rather than risk going out. Two young policemen were knocked out while the mob 'trumpeted its triumph'. Talk about exaggerate. Apparently the local police were 'out on their feet' anyway, trying to cope with these juvenile tearaways, these hoodlums, who were targeting law and authority.

The reporter couldn't even get the verbal stuff right. One youth (who hadn't brushed his teeth) was rocking backwards and forwards on his Cuban heels and demanding money: 'I ain't saying anything else without nicker, see? I reckon what I've got to say is worth twenty nicker, ain't it? Apiece, I mean!'

'Without nicker'. Without a pair of knickers, maybe.

I mean, that's what we are – working class. Gorblimey and strike a light, guv, you've got us bang to rights. Urchins, all of us. In one breath he says, 'It's a dead and alive hole,' then he says, 'There's plenty of amusement here, mate, and up to now we haven't paid for it. Tell that to the coppers, we'll take them any time.' Just who was this geezer? 'Coppers'? Not our language, I'm afraid. Got it wrong there as well. 'Cops' for a laugh sometimes, maybe, but 'Coppers'?

And then a police-dog handler arrived with Rin Tin Tin and shepherded the 'whooping' mob across the street. 'Big fucking deal,' they shouted. Except that 'fucking' had to be excluded from the report in case the British public who read it were offended. Yeah, these hoodlums, these thigh-booted, shade-wearing, whooping thugs swear too.

'These scooter riders are aged between sixteen and nineteen – and their girlfriends are even younger.'

Child-shagging whooping thugs.

But the reporter got it wrong when he said, 'Next year it could be any other seaside town. Where parents go down to the beach with bucket and spade,' because it was going to be next *bank holiday. This* year.

The prick even suggested that these whooping, thigh-booted, Cuban-heeled, shaded thugs knew more about sex and drugs than basic hygiene. Fucking steady on. Just what do these people think kids get up to?

But what we were all waiting to hear was this: 'The authorities have no answer to the hooliganism . . .'

Fucking great.

The head of Clacton's police bemoaned, 'I've got a teenage boy myself, but I don't understand. They come from decent homes.' Perhaps too decent, the report says. These animals respect nobody. They feel free to terrorise, as long as it's someone else's territory. An army without a cause. They believe in nothing, apparently.

Of course, they don't understand. Decent homes? What a joke. Decent homes where the kids are unwanted and left to fend for themselves while the parents fight to get their snouts in the trough of booming Britain before another war comes along and blows it all apart again. All my generation are fucking accidents, war-over, lucky-to-be-alive shagging accidents, products of bludgeoned, psychotic parents who were themselves the children of impoverished weirdos who thought that sex was disgusting and that killing your fellow man was normal, especially if he was foreign.

'Decent homes'. What the fuck does 'decent' mean, anyway? Touching your forelock to his lordship? Wringing your cap as you stand head-bowed before your master?

Bollocks.

You've got a bunch of kids here who won't do it. Kids who are going to create a ruck until the world sits up and takes notice. *We're* in charge now.

FIVE

BRIGHTON

Five of us – myself, Dinger, Mac, Russell and Martin – set out from London in Russell's convertible Mercedes. The roads were full of scooter boys and Rockers on motorbikes and other carloads of Mods, and the trains were likewise packed, with most of the passengers non-paying, heading out of London for Brighton or Margate.

Sheila had done some nice business in the West End and I was flush, but she was beginning to worry me. Dinger had noticed it too. It looked like she was going to branch out on her own. She'd already argued she wanted half, not a third, of the proceeds, and now she was saying she could do it single-handed, which both of us doubted. But apart from the risk to her, it meant that I had to start thinking about finding another source of income.

Actually, my instincts were telling me it was time for a change; we'd come very close to getting a pull when an old punter recognised us and began screaming abuse in Regent Street. Luckily he had a heart attack or something and collapsed on the pavement before he could draw too much attention to us, but it was worrying at the time. Then I was dragged into West End Central and knocked about for a bit until they realised they'd got the wrong person. So, naturally enough, I was beginning to feel uneasy; you can only get up to mischief for so long on one patch before they capture you, because as soon as your face becomes known people start asking questions and putting two and two together and coming up with all sorts of amazing things, and we had no cover story to keep them happy.

'What do you reckon on Sheila then?' asked Dinger, picking his nose.

'Nothing. As far as I'm bothered it's over. Why don't you leave it alone, you dirty bastard.'

Russell looked back. He modelled himself on a fifties film star, looking a bit like Alan Ladd crossed with one of the Chipmunks, and was never really one of us, being a bit older and more responsible. But he had good cars. 'Girlfriend trouble?' he asked. He was probably making sure Dinger wasn't smearing bogies on his car.

'Sort of. But I think I'll survive.'

'Will *she* though?' murmured Dinger. I think he was developing a crush on her, especially now he knew I wasn't interested. Usually, I'd have a go at anything, but she had a dodgy hooter, and I found it difficult to be attracted to females if they had flared nostrils. All the same, I liked her as a friend and it felt out of order that she should go it alone.

We drove into Brighton like high-ranking Nazi officers during the fall of Paris; funny how the war films on telly colour your impressions. Gangs of Mod troops stood about on corners, outside cafés and along the seafront, where we did a tour of inspection flanked by a score of scooters which had tagged on as we'd entered town. Cheers went up as Russell drove the Mercedes on to the pavement at Palace Pier and I jumped out with Dinger to join the gathering crowd.

Frankie was there sporting a new full-length red suede coat with red leather collar, cuffs and patch pockets, with a crew from Mile End and Stepney, and there were other contingents from Lewisham, Bromley, Woolwich, Dagenham, Ilford, Tottenham, Islington, Fulham and Clapham, as well as scores of other little groups who came from just about every corner of London and the surrounding areas. And they kept pouring in.

A gang of about twenty Rockers rode by to jeers and boos from the crowd, followed a few minutes later by an impressive drive-past of about fifty bikes, including someone at the front who looked very much like Kenser Donnelly. The atmosphere, already charged, began to intensify like it does in the movies when the curtains close over Pearl and Dean just before the big film.

Crossing the road, I found a vacant phone box outside the Aquarium Dance Hall and made a call to a friend in the Tahiti Club at Margate. He reported back that the same was happening there; the trouble had already started with a scooter boy being driven off the road by a gang of Rockers on the main road into town, and reprisals were already taking place, the Rockers being outnumbered by at least ten to one.

Back at the pier, I passed on the news that trouble had already started in Margate, and a surge of electricity went through the crowd as word passed around. On cue, another gang of Rockers rode in along the seafront to more jeers and catcalls from the crowds lining the road, and as they growled by on their machines the girls riding pillion responded with V signs and clenched fists. Most of the blokes were older, and they looked mean, but underneath all that leather and dirt they were just as vulnerable as anyone.

'Let's have the cunts!' shouted Frankie, getting fired up.

But the timing wasn't right and I had a better idea. 'Let's just all wander into town, split up into groups and reform here later. Spread the word around. By that time the Rockers will have parked up and will be off guard and we'll be able to swarm all over them.'

Crossing the promenade, we walked on up towards

West Street, which led towards the station, and turned off in towards town, leaving the rest behind.

The sun was shining, I had a pocketful of money, I felt confident and I was with real friends, friends that you met wherever you went, more often than not without arrangement. We were so close – yet entirely independent – that we each knew what everyone else was doing most of the time. And today we were all together, fearless, happy and carefree, knowing that the big moment had at last arrived when we could shove it in their faces and show just who we were.

Mods. We'd give 'em fucking middle-class Mods.

Outside Jaeger we met up with Lil the Pill and some of her mates who'd just got off the train, and Dinger got it into his head to show them the town, so we left him to it and went instead to the Lorelei, a basement café in The Lanes which was used by a few of the local beats. Here there were dozens more kids down from London, and we passed the word around to regroup by the Aquarium later. Pills were passed on, bought and sold, and I swallowed another half-dozen dexedrine to top up the dozen I'd taken a couple of hours earlier. Frankie was already grinding his jaws and I was talking meaningfully and non-stop to anyone within earshot, so we had to get mobile before speed complacency and time warp set in; there was always the danger with speed that, enraptured by your own words, you'd lose all sense of time and end up missing out on the action. You had to keep mobile to keep a grip.

We stood up from the table.

A little sort from Stratford asked where I was going. She was nice. Real smart. Black crop, red knitted top, black ski-pants and French gym shoes. But I'm off out. See you later, I said . . .

* * *

Check hair in mirror, check old Madras jacket, fine black knitted shirt with grey collar, pale yellow cotton strides and mustard, tasselled suede shoes from Raoul's (couldn't risk wearing a mohair suit with all the potential aggravation) – everything looks good. Ready.

Outside, the sun is still shining and Brighton is being kind. I love Brighton, beautiful Brighton, its pretty girls, the warm, London village atmosphere and tolerance.

Frankie, speeding ahead with his hands clasped behind his back under his suede coat, suddenly veers through the side door of a hotel and up the stairs. I follow. Out on to a landing, we check door handles, soundlessly twisting them as we go. One, carelessly locked, opens with just a bit of shoulder and we slide in and look about, but there's nothing there bar a pair of stockings and an empty cigarette packet on the sideboard.

But the door at the far end of the landing is unlocked and the room is taken, so we steal in nice and quiet after first peeping round the door to make sure no one's there. In front of the bay window stands a dresser, against one wall is a wardrobe, and dominating the room is a big double bed. From a door leading off you can hear a shower running and someone splashing about.

I close the door gently behind us as Frankie rifles a handbag on the dressing-table and skirt the bed to the wardrobe to check out the contents. Inside is a blue serge suit for a big bloke, a couple of dresses and a Fair Isle jumper which Frankie spots and pulls from the wardrobe to hold up against him for size. The shower noises now include the soft singing of a woman. A woman! I tip-toe to the door and put my eye to the gap, and there behind a frosted screen stands a female body. She turns off the shower and steps out of the cubicle just as I jump away from the door and hiss at Frankie, 'She's coming!' Automatically we dive under the bed and lie on our backs, staring up at the bedsprings as she sweeps into the bedroom, towelling herself dry. She sings the theme from *A Summer Place* – 'Laaaa de de de de, de de de deeeeee de de, diddle deee de de, diddle dooo' – as she finally drops the towel on to the floor and sits before the dressing mirror. All we can see is her legs. I turn my head to stare at Frankie and the deadpan expression on his face kills me, so I look away quickly and stare again at the bedsprings above, trying to think of something serious, like getting caught red-handed, but Frankie has picked up on it and I can feel his body shaking. But something very unfunny happens as suddenly the door clicks open and two large male shoes and cavalry twill trouser bottoms walk in.

We listen, now torn between hilarity and horror. He could be anyone. A professional boxer, a personal body-guard, Old Bill, one of the Crazy gang.

'All right, love?' he says to her with a murderer's voice. 'You should have locked the door, walking around like that. Anyone could have come in.'

Shit. I remember the handbag Frankie's been through. Pray she doesn't notice all the money's gone. Now I need a crap.

'Course they wouldn't. Don't be silly.'

'Mmm, you smell nice.'

Kissing sounds.

'It's Blue Grass. Do you like it?'

'Mmm . . .' Kissing sounds again. Naked female feet turn to face male shoes.

More kissing sounds. 'We've got an hour . . .'

Shirt falls to the floor, followed by vest. Big hands remove big male shoes. Trousers drop to floor as naked female feet pad round to my side of bed. Springs creak and the bed sags as female body lies down. Blue Y-fronts land a foot away from Frankie's face and he turns to look at me, screwing his face up in disgust. Male sits on edge of bed and removes socks, which he drops on top of Y-fronts, then lifts legs and turns to face female on bed.

Kissing starts again. Small gasps from her as he does something.

'That's nice,' she whispers, not knowing that my nose is inches from the small of her back. More kissing and loud breathing. Then, as we lie staring up, the pressure concentrates as they double up and the bed sinks closer. Quietly we wriggle to the edges of the bed to avoid contact.

A bigger gasp, then rhythmic movements which build up, slow down, build up, until female moaning begins, which changes to rhythmic gasps and moans building in pitch until she gives out a long, louder gasp and a little grunt.

Then sudden movement as the weight on bed redistributes itself into two areas again.

We wait, one minute, two minutes, five minutes . . . then snoring above. I look at Frankie. He nods his head towards the door and very, very slowly we start to slide out from beneath the bed, inch by inch, lift a shoulder, squirm, move leg slowly over, until we are clear of the bed, then slowly sit up; woman looks like Diana Dors, man looks like Victor Mature's big brother, she wheezing, he snoring. Tiptoe to the door, gently take handle, slip catch and, holding breath, CLICK!

Loud gasp from the bed, then a shriek, then Victor Mature's brother grumbling, 'What's going on?' She screams 'Look!' and he jumps up, his bollocks flailing about, and Frankie turns, scared but cool, to face him. With a gun in his hand. A fucking *gun* in his hand! Vic stops in mid-step like an ice-age mammoth. Di has her hand clamped to her mouth, eyes extremely wide open.

'Sorry about this,' says Frankie, 'but we've come into the wrong room.'

Vic's jaw drops. 'Wrong room?' He takes a step forward.

'Stay right where you are, or you'refuckingdead!' says Frankie with an amphetamine rush which makes the last three words join together and roar out too loud.

I open the door, wanting to laugh but too scared, and we ease ourselves out, then bolt down the stairs. The door bursts open behind us and Vic gives chase, clutching a pink towel to his nuts. 'Stop!' he bellows and the hotel manager comes at us in the foyer, but Frankie holds him off with the gun and we flee out into the street laughing hysterically as the rest of the world watches the build-up of Mods and Rockers along the seafront.

Back into The Lanes. 'Where the fuck did you get that gun?' I ask.

'It's a starting pistol. You can buy them anywhere.'

'Show us.' I examine the heavy black thing, dying to pull the trigger. 'Let's do a bank.'

'It's Saturday.'

'A jeweller's then.' I stick the starting pistol in my pocket, feeling extraordinarily powerful. Speed and a gun. What more could a young man want?

Crowds of British Home Stores holidaymakers pushing bland ice-cream into their faces are jostling their way through the narrow alleys as we look for a suitable jeweller's – something small, off the beaten track, run by a lone cripple, where I can practise my James Cagney imitation – and eventually we find it. As we enter, a sprung bell on the door jangles, announcing our arrival, and an old man with a velvet smoker's jacket and a round hat with a tassel turns to welcome us. 'Afternoon, boys, what can I do for you?' he asks in a kindly voice.

I explain in Cagney-voice that I'm looking for a watch, preferably second-hand . . .

'With a second hand,' says the old man.

'No, you old prick,' says Frankie, laughing, looking about for something worth stealing. 'Second-hand. You know what I mean. Not new. Someone's had it before.' He's still laughing, so the old man, probably thinking he's misheard the term 'old prick', assumes he's being pleasant.

He chuckles indulgently like old cunts do. 'Oh, I see, I see. Well, let me think.'

'Hurry up about it,' adds Frankie, doing Edward Gee Robinson to a tee.

I crease up.

'Now then, I had a nice French one come in this morning.' He searches about under the counter and pulls out a watch. 'Here it is. Patek Phillipe.'

'Show me,' I say, tears running down my cheeks.

And he hands it over as I pull the gun on him.

Staring long and hard at the gun as if he can't believe his eyes, he looks up at me in confusion. Everything hangs in these seconds and I'm still laughing when I look into his watery old eyes. If he'd played on it, come on with the sympathy or the 'I was young once' number, I'd have probably put the gun away and said it was all a joke, but he blew it.

'Don't be a fool,' he snaps, like a schoolteacher.

So, taking a step back, I shout, 'Okay! Get your hands up and don't try anything or I'll fill you full of holes, Granpaw!'

Frankie starts laughing and can't stop; the old man at first raises his hands then lowers them in disbelief; so I walk round behind the counter, push him out of the way and take the notes from the old wooden till.

'I say, I say,' he complains bitterly.

So I aim the gun and shoot him for the hell of it, and we run out laughing as a middle-aged couple come in, surprised but smiling politely.

Down at Palace Pier, meanwhile, a good crowd of a few hundred kids has formed, all waiting for action. A big band of Rockers has gathered just off the seafront and they are sitting about on their machines taking the piss out of the rest of the world and frightening the pensioners. Dinger's there at the fore, stirring the crowd, just as Frankie and I arrive running. The energy passes from us and everyone starts running, sending up a cry of 'Rockers!' as they charge across the road.

But instead of running, the Rockers, who are out-numbered ten to one, stand their ground, looking ready for a fight. We come to a halt twenty feet away and begin a verbal confrontation.

The leader of the Rockers, a caveman with a beautiful girlfriend who needs converting, keeps walking a few paces towards us, offering us out, and withdrawing. He spits on the ground in contempt. 'Come on!' he screams. 'Any five of you! Any ten of you!'

Then an empty Coke bottle arcs through the air and shatters on his tousled head. Down he goes, and we charge. At least, the rest charge, and kick shit out of the Rockers – the Mod girls, by the way, are a lot tougher than the Rocker girls, who have to be nice and girly for their butch boyfriends – while I hover about on the edge of the battle-ground with Frankie, having a smoke and counting out money.

Within minutes the Rockers are routed; some have run, while others have somehow managed to jump on their bikes and escape, leaving the girls to fight it out. When the action is finally over, the Brighton police, shrewd as they are, still haven't shown. A bike lies burning on its side and a score of bruised and bleeding leather-clad bodies are lying groaning in the road. But, more importantly, a dance is about to start in the Aquarium Dance Hall and I drop another dozen pills to make sure I don't come down too soon.

Under the arches along the lower road from the Aquarium, the scooter boys have made camp in rows and rows, their sleeping bags laid out on carefully requisitioned pieces of ground ready for the night. But apart from posing about and trying to look superior, they are captives of their own lifestyle, many of them refusing to leave their bikes. Most are doubtful dressers, being impoverished after paying for the bikes (unless they were paid for by mum and dad, which many are), and there is a rift, just a tiny rift, between them and everyone else because some of them fancy their chances just a little bit too much.

Someone's brought a portable record player and a beach party is starting, the smoke from the driftwood fire curling up into the air and mingling with the smell of candyfloss, fish and chips and seaweed. Frankie Ford is singing 'Sea Cruise' as twilight descends and the pier begins to show its true colours, like an exotic nocturnal sea creature luring plankton into its gaping mouth. The sea hisses gently through the pebbles in the background, and for this brief moment a heavy peace settles over the town.

A little while later and the Aquarium Dance Hall is beginning to thump, the entrance and the road outside packed with blocked kids talking about the victory. I've slipped away to meet a group of Brighton girls I met at Easter to supply them with speed, and they're great: up front with the cash, pills straight down their necks, no questions. But they've brought friends who want some as well and people are beginning to notice, so I arrange to meet them on the lower seafront walkway in half an hour.

Dropping another half-dozen to lift the buzz just that bit more, I stroll back past the crowds at the Aquarium before passing through the tunnel under the promenade to the beach. I sit on a bench, stick a Piccadilly in my mouth, strike a light, breathe in that wonderful smoke, but I badly want to talk to someone. Johnny from Bromley materialises with Alan G and they buy pills with the cash they've just lifted from an old queer in the public lavatories. Johnny lures them in, and Alan rolls them. Works every time.

'Heard the Old Bill's about,' says Johnny.

'They're going to raid the Aquarium,' adds Alan.

They're warning me about dealing down there. 'I've only got a few left on me, and they're spoken for,' I say.

But then a group of police appear along the walkway – you can see their white helmets a mile off – and we melt quickly back into the crowd.

Inside the dance hall everyone's doing their thing, whichever dance happens to be fashionable, or just standing around, but nobody's seen Dinger. Mac's with a local girl, like a snake with a rabbit. Frankie's over-pilled in the corner, talking about glassing some geezer who's Old Bill in disguise; he looks a bit unstable to me so I slide away, not being in the mood for violence, and suddenly run into the smart little sort from Stratford I met in the Lorelei. She's got a couple of geezers hanging around but I don't care and ask if she fancies coming for a walk along the seafront.

Outside the main doors we squeeze through the crowds but before we can get right out there is a surge of bodies and shouts and screams as an army of police rush in. They make random arrests and seal off the upper exits to check everyone leaving.

I look at the Stratford sort. 'What did you say your name was?' I ask.

'Mo,' she says. 'What's yours when you're at home?'

'Tommy. Look, there's a little problem here. Come in this phone box.' I pull open the door and we get in.

'What?' she asks.

Police are standing right outside.

'I've got . . .' – I look into a brown envelope and do a quick stock take – '. . . thirty-two dexies left. I don't really want to swallow the lot. D'you want some?'

She glances outside. 'I don't know whether I could manage without a drink. How many have you got to get rid of?'

'About a dozen.' I try to work out how many I've taken so far, but can't. 'Go in and buy a Coke. Here's the money.'

She laughs. 'Are you joking?'

'No. Just say to the Old Bill on the door that you've left your purse on the bar; be polite and they'll let you in and out. Leave your bag here, then if you get a pull I'll come to the rescue with your handbag. They're all right with couples.'

'Why shouldn't I just say I'm going back in for a Coke? There's nothing wrong with that.'

'While they're raiding the place? They'll think you're taking the piss.'

She sees what I'm getting at and goes off for a Coke, entirely happy to leave her bag with me.

Inside is a season ticket to Tower Hill (she probably works in the City), photos of her and friends leering into the camera, a purse with about four pounds in it, some letters, Kleenex tissues, old dance tickets for the Tottenham Royal and the Lyceum, a well-worn address book and a couple of biros, a steel comb with a sharp handle, lipstick and other make-up, and a wicked-looking hatpin with a cut-glass top. She knows how to protect herself then.

Five minutes later, while I've pretended to make a call, she comes back with two ice-cold Cokes and downs twelve pills while I swallow the last twenty.

The police raid is well planned and over as quickly as it started, before any retaliation can begin, and we walk out.

Outside are Russell and Martin in Gestapo Supercar, trying to look cool, but the car is beating them hands down. I look at Mo. 'Where you staying tonight?' I ask, as my brain begins to veer off track, out of control on sudden speed overload. 'D'you fancy coming up the Flamingo?'

'Tonight? By the time we get up there it'll be all over. I've got a tent with a friend up at Black Rock – there's a lot of us up there. Why don't you come back? Someone said there was going to be a party with a bonfire and all that; it'd be really nice if you came back, you could share the tent; my mate wouldn't mind, we've only got two sleeping bags, but my mate probably won't be there because she said she might be going back to some geezer's flat and, well, I'm sure it'll be warm enough . . .'

Speed's kicking in with her all right as well. 'Russ!' I shout. 'Take us up to Blackheath.'

'Black Rock. What's up there?'

'Everyone's camping up there – I don't fancy kipping on the beach.'

As if I'm going to kip anywhere.

But I try to hide the speed thing from Russell because he won't understand. But he must know now because I'm chewing air, talking bollocks, beginning to foam at the mouth and listing to one side like the *Titanic.*

'Come on then,' he shouts back, looking a bit nervous.

Mo is impressed, and we're chauffeured to Black Rock, but by the time we get there I have no idea what is happening and keep thinking I'm back in London, accusing Russell of tricking us. Russell gets more worried and drives away, leaving us in a vast sea of darkness surrounded by glowing green-and-blue triangles. Mo grasps my hand and guides me as I try to avoid a red double-decker bus which flies by ten feet in the air followed by a man on a bike, but she insists I'm seeing things. My balance is affected and I collapse on an occupied triangle, then she helps me into another one where I collapse on my back in the gloom, unsure if I'm standing up in the Wall of Death or lying down. Suddenly she starts snogging me and pulling my willy and this goes on for hours and hours and hours and I'm back at school and then at home with the dog, who's growling at me then licking my mouth out, then I'm getting caught wanking in front of the class and getting told off by Toni the Greek and Nicole, then being marched naked before a screaming mob who want to crucify me, and my heart is pumping itself dry, and I try again and again to get it in but it keeps bending and please help me God I'll never take speed again and my muscles are in torment all over and the nerve-endings are electric and I'm shivering and freezing hot and biting her face off and my tongue is painful and black shadows flit in and out of my closed eyes until the utterly depressing finality of a cold grey light poisons the blackness to reveal the dawning monstrosity of yet another new day.

Fuck. I feel so fucking guilt-ridden miserable. Caked mouth bone dry taste of stale blood eyes dry bones aching head like a vast empty cave.

Trousers are off somewhere and my tortured penis is very cold. She, also half-naked, is using my jacket as a pillow and is dribbling all over it and talking and blubbering in her half-sleep. I can't bear it. Suicide is the only way out. I'd cry if she wasn't there.

Some fucking cunt outside is playing with his scooter, revving it up. What's the fucking point of it all?

Gently lifting her head with shaking hands to avoid waking her and having to communicate, I take my jacket, find my trousers – which are filthy and grass-stained – put them on, then my shoes, and creep out of the tent into the maddening half-light.

And I walk, trying to hang on to the tightrope that is my sanity, knowing that one wrong thought could make me lose balance forever and fall into something terrifying.

Stare at the grass, but its green violence shocks me, then when I look away everything is red. I can't escape it. I can't get away from my own head. Red, green, red, green, red, green. Close the eyes but hopelessness floods back in.

I must do something about it. I must. Now, before it's too late.

Run. Run. Out on to the road.

Just the sound of distant shoes clumping on the tarmac. Breathing fast, cool air, watering eyes. Clump, clump, clump, clump. This is good. But can I bear to stop? The closeness of the pumping blood. The nose before my vision. The heat inside, the cold outside. Looking down at my filth. Looking up at the purple sky. Looking around at the dead-eyed houses.

To run is to survive. To keep one step ahead of perception.

Clump, clump, clump . . .

And back into town.

Slow down and walk now. Insanity alone is one thing, but insanity observed . . .

Along the seafront the misery of the dawn is stirring the sleepers; fashion icons separated from their composure stagger about unwashed and foul-breathed, asking if anyone knows where to get a cup of tea. But this is England, the land of the dead, and the only tea is that being drunk indulgently by those with enough foresight to bring along camping gear or a flask, those boring tossers who, in their teens, are already showing that smug organisational trait that once made England great and now threatens to turn it into a mausoleum. These cunts will undermine our movement, stifle its reactionary soul.

The pointlessness of it all is devastating. Why does the cold tide bother to come in and go out? Does anyone hear the tiny pebble chattering as it swishes backwards and forwards to oblivion? Oh God, why was I born?

Is there anything left to dream of?

Even dreams are frightening, with their empty promises and delusion, for a dream is but a dream, and when they become reality they die . . .

'Tommeeee!' A voice breaks into my head. Across the promenade Dinger and Lil the Pill are sitting close together on a low wall. I wander across, too ill to care about appearances, but attempting to walk steadily. Which makes me misjudge the kerb and uneven road surface so that I stagger like one of the brain-dead.

'Look at the fucking state of you. Your flies are undone,' says Dinger. 'Where have you been?'

I want to vomit. The strain of having to talk is almost impossible to handle. I begin to reply but the thought of the words 'Black' and 'Rock' make me heave, and I eject green slime from my stomach on to the pavement.

Lil makes sounds of sympathy as the first sunrays begin to chase the shadows away and I see a tiny rainbow in a bubble of spit. Now I'm retching air and my head is spinning and I cannot face either of them because they are too grotesque; their faces horrify my Big Dipper brain which is plunging downwards.

Dinger is a Bosman's Potto.

'I gotta go,' I hear my head say, and I follow it away along the seafront towards Hove. Clump, clump, clump, clump . . .

'Hove!' I hear myself say aloud.

Hove frightens me. The word reminds me of toast and margarine and slightly cheesy, leathery socks and warm minges, talcum powder and cosy buttocks, something

101

terrifyingly seedy; one of the many orifices of England around which clinker clusters.

I suddenly hate England and its vicious complacency, its smug fucking defiance in the face of change. This is the land of nice people who take tea who, with your best interests in mind, advise you how to live but despise you if you don't do it their tried and tested way; cold and super-ficial social climbers, who mistrust even their own children.

They mistrust even their own children.

I know my parents don't trust me.

They despise me.

They must, because they keep wanting me to be someone else. To be like them or their fucking film stars.

They only wanted the best for me, they said once in a moment of bitterness.

But . . .

Aren't I the best one to decide what's best for me?

And now, because of their meddling, their trying to get in on my act, I've deliberately blown everything just to make sure they couldn't claim any credit for my success.

I remember as a small child . . .

Fuck this uneven pavement . . .

I remember as a small child the . . .

Exuberant but shallow congratulations . . .

When I did something meaningless like take a shit, or stagger a few steps across the kitchen, or eat my food.

When I passed my eleven-plus they bought me a watch and paraded me about. When I left school and began thinking for myself they called me a cunt.

So cunt I'll be.

And cunt I am. If they don't like it, so much the better. I am my own cunt. My own grown-up, adult, brilliant, fucking cunt.

I must not, cannot, be . . . like them – other people's cunts.

Keep walking, ignoring the buildings on the right where dreadful things are beginning to happen: where glaring white teeth are being taken from overnight glasses, and ointments and unctions are being rubbed lovingly into waxy flesh. Where beige socks with brown motifs are being pulled over misshapen feet, and large, boiled underpants with elastic fatigue are being checked for the possibility of a second wearing. Brilliantine, with its deathly smell, is being rubbed into worn hands and applied to thinning hair, as ammonia-stinking rollers are uncurled from dead locks that last blew free in the wind years before I was born.

These mortals and their offspring tell me how to live my life and I resent it; they don't have my knowledge of the universe, they can't see through my eyes. I am youth, the unknown quantity, and to be like them would be to die.

Badly need a drink. My mouth is like a venus fly trap. Hope no one's seen me burbling like a lunatic. But who gives a fuck anyway.

'Public Convenience,' says the sign.

Inside is a refuge of white tiles, chrome and running water. Even clean towels on a roller machine and paper for wiping your arse.

Strip to underpants.

Wash hands, wash arms, wash head, wash feet, wash armpits, wash crutch.

Have problem drying crutch due to height of towel machine. Towel machine crashes to floor, narrowly missing feet; easier now, if I hold it down with one foot while pulling the towel out.

Sponge stains on strides with damp bog roll.

Throw underpants and socks in bin. Get dressed again, adjust hair, finger-brush teeth and gargle.

Check money – still flush.

No pills. Good. That's the last time.

Thank God I'm still sane, but get frightened thinking about sanity, so look quickly at black-and-white tiles to change focus.

Cleaner now and feeling much better, but still viciously depressed.

Early-morning old cunt comes in and says 'Lovely day' in that accent that means he's spent half his life with his head stuck up someone else's arse and he thinks he's better than me.

Get out quick before I lose my mind again. He'll probably report me for vandalising the towel machine, get me arrested and tortured, fucking cunt.

Don't like shoes with no socks – they clump more – or strides with no underpants – might get shit on them.

Walk back towards Brighton now, as everything's getting worse as I walk further west. Signs of industrial carnage and work.

Now some traffic starting. Signs of life instead as new day gets people buzzing from place to meaningless place. Turn inland into town centre, see clock and it says nine. The world begins at nine. Find café and have tea.

Tea stirs up old speed momentarily and I have a short buzz followed by another comedown. Attempt sausage sandwich, knowing that to eat will do me good, but it causes vomit juice to flood into my mouth and I have to drop it and stay dead still for very long three minutes until nausea subsides. Now café is closing in and I feel everyone is secretly observing me. Can I get out without screaming, dying or creating some sort of disturbance? Or should I sit and wait until everyone is gone? No. There is no lavatory here where I can hide.

Nothing for it but to rejoin the others and brazen it out.

There is a very strong air of the morning after the night before as we all gather along the seafront. There must be thousands of us, and a few Rocker conversions with swiftly restyled hair meekly drifting along with the tumbleweed like stray camouflaged elks in a pack of wolves. But another confrontation is looking likely as gangs of bikers keep pouring into town. Despite yesterday's defeat and encouraged by increasing numbers, they are beginning to park closer and closer to the front again, where we are gathered, instead of hiding along the far end of the seafront, so I phone Margate and pass it on that we need back-up here in Brighton.

Then the skirmishes begin and we keep winning – mainly because we outnumber them, but also because we keep the beach as our base. With the sea behind us we only have one front to fight on and a lot of stones to throw, and whenever they get near, the stones send them scattering in retreat. That's when we charge. Simple. But don't get caught wandering about by yourself.

I don't think anyone can believe our conviction.

To throw one egg-sized stone across the promenade is unthinkable, dreadful, my dear, but volleys of them that darken the sky, well – everyone's outraged and astonished.

And what's it all about?

Forget your psychiatrists and psychologists and police experts and educated column writers. None of them know. It's about something few, if any, of them could understand – the knowledge that we are the children of a new age.

And we are euphoric and invincible.

Rockers aren't children of the new age, they're products of the old and they have to go, it's as simple as that.

It's the new versus the old – and the police can't cope.

* * *

At midday, the public houses opened and, for me at least, a new era began: I tasted beer and liked it – not for the first time, but for the first time on a speed comedown during a riot. Slowly, as I drank half pint after half pint of bitter ale, the depression lifted, humour re-entered my life and confidence poured back in. When the publican barred us for throwing empties at Rockers, we smashed the windows in.

From there we moved on to another seafront pub where the landlord was more sympathetic and boosted his takings beyond his wildest dreams.

Despite the periodic routs of the Rockers, there came a stage in the early afternoon when a stand-off took place as the sun and the beer relaxed everyone. Rumours of Rocker reinforcements went around on both sides, and some bikers began to roar around again as if the ultimate victory was going to be theirs.

Rave on, it's a crazy feeling . . .

Then a wonderful and stirring thing happened. Glasses of beer in hand, sitting watching the Rockers strutting about on the other side of the road, we all slowly became aware of a strange distant hum. Silence fell as everyone stopped talking, and the sound grew louder and louder. Across the road the bikers stood like statues, staring up the coast road to the east, wondering what was coming.

Then came a glint from the crest of the hill as at first one, then two, then four, then eight and finally hundreds of scooters poured into town from Margate, rank after rank of chromed and coppered scooters riding abreast the entire width of the road.

An almighty cheer went up, which turned into a battle-cry as the Rockers were rushed and put to flight. Running leather-clad figures once again disappeared beneath the flailing feet of dozens of attackers. Mod girls battered Rocker girls, police ran for shelter and grannies cheered us on. Cafés and pubs that had been hostile were ransacked, and Kenser Donnelly and his gang were battered and run out of town.

Final victory had come. After all this time, the reigning champions had been annihilated.

After the battle came relaxation, sunbathing and swimming. Some took to diving into the sea fully dressed; others stripped off, cheered on by crowds of holidaymakers.

With the Rockers gone we could relax and enjoy ourselves, and everybody else did too: families on the beach mixed and played ballgames with us as toddlers shrieked with happiness, coachloads of grannies showed their drawers as they did the 'knees up' with gangs of brightly coloured London kids outside seafront pubs, and for the first time in years you could walk around a seaside town on a bank holiday without having to cast your eyes downwards every time you met a gang of bikers flexing their muscles by the side of the road.

Then, with priceless timing, hundreds of police reinforcements came in to control a situation that had been and gone, causing another one to take its place – that of Law and Order versus Mods. The Clacton bogey had returned, and they were going to get their own back.

That afternoon the police unwittingly joined forces with the defeated Rockers, guaranteeing trouble for the future. No doubt someone important had decided that the damned Mods ought to be shown who was boss and that it was a matter of national pride and all that bollocks. And besides, you didn't want the peasants to get any ideas, did you?

Already the reporters were streaming into town, hungry for sensation at the expense of truth. The relaxed attitude of the Brighton police up until that moment had been seen as a failure of duty, whereas if the truth be known they were the only ones to get it right.

Now, stones began to rain down on them.

But the great thing was that we'd won back our identity; our strategy had worked. The Mod thing really was no longer seen as middle class, but working class. One hundred per cent.

Well, well.

That evening I met Sherri, as gorgeous as ever, walking along with her friend Rose. They'd come down with a group of friends and relatives for a blues party in a hired church hall and Sherri asked if I would like to come along.

'Only if you come for a little walk with me first,' I said, ever hopeful.

She looked all schoolmarmish then. 'And where would you be wanting to walk?'

'Anywhere. I don't mind. Around town. Along the seafront. I'll show you the sights. Where do you fancy?' For added decency I then said that Rose was welcome to come too. What was happening? Decency wasn't usually my thing.

'How about if we go and see The Lanes? Do you know them?'

'Yeah, of course I do. All right, where shall we meet?'

Rose quickly said she couldn't come because she had to help her dad unpack, bless her, and I said 'You sure?', hoping she wouldn't change her mind.

'Why don't you bring some of your friends?' asked Sherri.

'What, for a walk?'

She laughed that lovely squeaky laugh. 'No, silly, to the dance.'

Back on the seafront, I told Dinger and Mac about the blues party. The alternative was another do in the Aquarium Dance Hall and both of them were on promises. There

108

was also another beach party in the offing which would see us through the night after everything was shut, so we agreed to meet up there if we didn't meet earlier.

As arranged, I met Sherri at the clocktower and we went strolling in the evening sunshine, down through The Lanes, stopping at the Lorelei for a cup of coffee. From there we made our way towards the seafront and ran straight into a small bunch of Rockers quietly leaving town, but instead of stopping to have a go at me, as I expected, they drove by pulling faces and making monkey noises at Sherri. Before I could say anything, she burst into laughter.

I stared at her. 'What are you laughing for? Don't that piss you off?' I asked.

'I was laughing at your face – you looked so . . . mad.'

She was like that, so happy all the time.

And race discrimination wasn't all one way, as I was to find out later.

The dance was held in an old church hall and was just about big enough to hold everyone by the time Dinger and Mac and their girls and then Frankie and a few mates and a couple of dozen others turned up out of the blue, and everything seemed set for a rare evening. Rose's uncle, the DJ, had an excellent collection of imported ska records, many of which we'd never heard before, and everybody danced together like one big family for most of the evening. Some of the local girls who'd come along with Frankie and had never heard the music before were so taken up with it that they cleared the floor temporarily until they managed to relax into the rhythm and stop battering everyone. Then, just as things levelled out nicely, 'Madness' came on and Dinger went right over the top with his version of the ska, causing Sherri to collapse on me in a fit of hysterical laughter.

Rose's cousin Leroy didn't like this very much and was the only one who didn't contribute to the general air of exuberance which filled the hall that night. When Derek Harriot's 'Wedding Song' came on he almost blew a gasket glaring at us through the gloom as we slowly danced cheek to cheek, and I could feel him cursing me for intruding on what he saw as his exclusive territory. Later, keeping well aware of his movements in case he turned nasty, I noticed him quietly leave the hall only to return a few minutes later, and when, about half an hour after, I saw the self-righteous smirk on his face as the police stormed in and rounded up the whites, I knew he'd been busy on the phone.

Two of the local kids were arrested for possession of pills and the party came to a premature end, causing bad feeling all round. But Leroy capped it by accusing us white trash of spoiling the reputation of his dear coloured folk who'd only come out for the day to enjoy themselves and spread a little happiness. Sherri told him not to be so stupid, and brother Neville eventually had to drag him away to stop him mouthing off and causing a riot, but I couldn't help feeling mad knowing that he'd caused all the problems just to get at me, then used the colour angle as a useful cover.

Before we white trash wandered off into the night I spoke to Sherri and told her of the beach party, but she thought it unlikely she'd be able to make it as they were going back to London with the coach at half past midnight. It was now just after 10.15 p.m.

'Look, try and make it,' I said. 'I need to see you on your own. But if I don't, watch out for Leroy, he's bad news.' I didn't want to say that I'd seen him leaving the hall just before the Old Bill arrived in case I'd got it all wrong.

'Don't worry about him, he's been chasing me since I

110

was a little girl and he was a skinny little boy. Neville keeps him at bay.'

'But will you try and get along to the party?' I asked, grabbing her hand.

She stood and thought about it for a few moments, pursing her beautiful lips. Then she appeared to make up her mind and asked where it was.

'On the beach a hundred yards from Palace Pier,' I said. 'By the Aquarium. You can't miss it – there'll be a fire and loads of people. Should be a right laugh.'

'I'll try, but after this drug thing I don't know – Dad's really upset.'

'It wasn't anything to do with us. The two geezers were strangers; they had tagged along with the girls Frankie brought along.'

We stood staring at each other for a bit, then, unsure of myself because she seemed a bit old-fashioned when it came to physical contact, I squeezed her hand and was about to say goodbye politely when Neville came along.

'Er, excuse me,' he said. 'I hope I'm not interrupting anything.'

'Like what?' said Sherri indignantly.

He smiled, then looked at me. 'Tommy, don't make too much of what happened here tonight – a few of us know Leroy of old, and we think we know where he went earlier on, but . . .'

I stopped him going any further. 'It's all right, he's just got it in for me because I like your sister. I just don't like the way he goes about it, that's all.'

'I know what you mean,' he said, then, as he was about to walk away, he stopped and added, 'We go training three nights a week, him and me – boxing training. You should come along. Maybe you could teach him some respect.' Then he grinned and walked away.

Boxing training? Yeah, and get my pretty face damaged? No thank you very much.

Without thinking, I leaned forward to kiss Sherri goodnight, and to my amazement she responded in a way that I suddenly felt I didn't deserve. Could she really like me this much? Surely not, I was a white citizen, third class.

Her breasts pressed against my chest and her tongue found mine, and not since the first open-mouthed kiss at the age of thirteen, when I'd gone to the pictures with a girl with real tits, had I felt this way. There came an urge in me so strong that she opened her eyes with a start and pulled away – my knob had come to life. Surely she knew what an erection was? She couldn't be that unworldly. Glancing down with a sparkle in her eye, she said, 'I think it's time I was going.'

I do believe I was embarrassed, and tried to laugh it off. 'Sorry,' I said, feeling that an apology might neutralise the implications of an erect dick, 'but it's your fault. I just can't help it.'

And she laughed again, that squeaky little laugh that was so fucking sexy. 'Don't apologise – I've got brothers. I've seen it all before. But I'd better go before I do something I shouldn't.'

Then she blew a kiss and walked away.

'You can! You can!' I shouted after her. 'I don't mind . . .'

She turned for an instant, gave another little smile, then walked into the hall.

Feeling extraordinarily pleased with myself, I ran the half-mile or so to the seafront and caught up with the rest. In the distance, a bonfire could be seen burning on the beach. Around it was a crowd of maybe a hundred, singing, dancing, shouting, laughing, kissing and cuddling, falling over, arguing, drinking and generally doing all the things that people do around a fire in the dark.

As I made my way into the crowd, a silhouette approached and put its face in mine – the silhouette of Mo from Stratford.

'Hello, stranger,' she said. 'Where did you get to?'

'Mo,' I laughed. 'Fuck . . .'

'If you like,' she joked. 'If you think you could manage it.' And she was still coming on strong, even after the disaster of the night before, despite the dig.

'I was out of my head. I worked it out – I did sixty dexies. Should have been pumped out.'

'Looked like it as well, the way you were carrying on. Can you remember what you were doing?'

'No?'

She smiled cheekily. At least if Sherri didn't turn up I had someone to keep me warm, I thought. She put her arm through mine.

'You were a very naughty boy,' she said.

No way. There's no way I could have shagged anyone. 'Why? What did I do?'

'I'm not telling you.'

After Sherri, I wasn't in the mood for this. 'Don't fuck about. What happened?'

Happy at seeing me worried, she then revealed that, apart from pissing over someone's Lambretta and running around the camping ground naked from the waist down, I'd also kicked a hole in her friend's dad's tent.

I couldn't remember running around like that. Fuck. I was lucky, then. Lucky to get away with it.

As if reading my thoughts, she added, 'It was a good job I was there, or else you'd have run back into town like it. I had to get someone to help me drag you back into the tent. For what good it was to anybody.'

'Well, I'm not pilled up tonight, so you'd better watch out,' I said quickly, trying to recover some of my dignity. Then I remembered Sherri and changed the subject.

By midnight, Dinger had crept off with Lil, Mac had taken his girl home, Frankie was conspiring with someone in the shadows under the pier and I was still trying to keep Mo at a respectable distance in case Sherri turned up, but knowing that the coach would be leaving at 12.30, I eventually gave up.

SIX

DISASTER

Around half midnight Frankie staggered across towards us, looking like something out of Dracula's castle in the flickering light from the fire, and I wondered what he was going to say. He could see that I was getting it on with Mo.

Blocked again, he stared intently at me as if he wanted to say something but couldn't. 'Er,' he began, searching for words, 'your . . . black mate . . . was here a couple of minutes ago.'

He was trying to be discreet. So Sherri had come along after all. Fuck. Had she seen me? Thoughts raced through my head: have I blown it? Should I try and get to the coach somehow? There was no point in hiding anything from Mo because she was only a casual acquaintance. She had no say in it.

'What do you mean "here"? Where was she?'

'I was over there,' he said, indicating towards the shadowy area where the tunnel went beneath the road to the Aquarium, 'and she came down the ramp looking for someone. You, I suppose. She started crossing the beach towards you, saw you two lusting and ran off back up towards town. You got a snout?'

I passed him a cigarette. So she had seen me. 'How long ago did you say?' I asked.

'About five, ten minutes.'

A funny thing happened just then. The fire died right down and a vague chill in the air caused me to shiver.

People started making excuses and wandering off, and I felt a huge, inexplicable sadness suddenly developing inside me. I wanted to cry. Surely this black sort wasn't affecting me that deeply? No, it was just the comedown; what did I expect after sixty pills?

I jumped up. 'Wait here,' I said to Mo, and ran off. If I could run fast enough, I might just catch the coach before it left; it was worth a try. Up the ramp I pounded, across the intersection, past the Pavilion and on up into the backstreets towards the station. I wondered how I would explain Mo away.

But what's it to do with anybody, after all, what I get up to? I'm not exactly going out with anyone.

Maybe she's so old-fashioned that she needs total commitment from me before I get any from her, or maybe a kiss to her is a contract.

Thoughts raced through my head one after the other as I dashed up the hill.

But the coach had gone and the church hall, dark and empty, mirrored my heart. I knew a major comedown from the speed was due but didn't really want it to happen right now. The booze had delayed it for a while but now I badly needed sleep, feeling suddenly and inexplicably overcome by exhaustion.

As I began the walk back, my legs shaking almost uncontrollably beneath me, I tried the handles of parked cars, one after another, until eventually I found one unlocked. Clambering in, I curled up on the back seat and began dreaming tumultuous, mad, helter-skelter dreams.

The noise of traffic and people walking by woke me early the next day. At first I wasn't sure where I was, but slowly it came back and I got out of the car before I was discovered by the owner. The sense of foreboding I'd felt the night before had passed, and I put it down to a combination of tiredness and disappointment at screwing up the meeting with Sherri.

Back down on the front, even larger crowds from London were already gathering for a last-day showdown with the Rockers, who were coming in again, but apart from the social side and the prospect of new talent being about, I was losing interest in any further confrontation with them; the deciding battles had taken place and the issue had been resolved. They'd lost. All I could see ahead was a period of skirmishing until the last of them called it a day and disappeared from the face of the earth. All these newcomers to the scene could do the clearing up, because I had a weird feeling that my life was about to change.

After cleaning up for the second morning running in a public lavatory, I drifted about through the crowds looking for Dinger or Mac or Frankie, but nobody had seen them. One vague piece of news that had an unpleasant ring to it was that someone, a girl, had been found halfway up Preston Street with bad head injuries, but that was no more than rumour. I made my way back up into town and went to the Lorelei, where I found Mo and Frankie sitting together like a pair of lovebirds.

As soon as I walked in I could sense something wasn't right and guessed straight away that they'd paired off when I hadn't returned last night, but I knew he couldn't have shagged her because he'd been too blocked. I bought a cup of tea and sat down with them.

'How's it going?' I asked, to get the ball rolling, as neither of them seemed willing to talk.

Mo smiled weakly but said nothing. Frankie stared me in the eye. 'You heard?' he asked.

'Heard what?'

'Lil's in hospital with head injuries, and Dinger's fucked off. He's done a runner.'

'What!' So she was the girl they'd found in Preston Street. This was unbelievable. 'Dinger's done a runner? What do you mean?'

'The Old Bill are looking for him. And you.'

'What are they looking for me for?'

'Well, I don't fucking know, do I? To eliminate you from their enquiries, I suppose,' he joked half-heartedly. 'They've been questioning everyone. Where have you been all night anyway – with that black sort?'

'No,' I said, 'she'd already gone.' Then it occurred to me that I couldn't prove where I'd been all night. Not that it mattered; I hadn't done anything. 'I slept in a car all night. I went looking for her but, as I said, she'd already gone, so I found an unlocked motor and kipped in it.'

'You'd better tell the Old Bill that. It's you or Dinger they think did it.'

'Me? What, because we're friends – are you fucking joking? Lil can tell them I didn't do it.'

'She's in a coma,' said Mo.

'Fucking hell, I don't believe this! We've got to find Dinger then. You got any idea where he's gone?'

'No. The best thing you can do – if you didn't do it – is get along to the nick, otherwise they'll put a warrant out for you and it'll get worse,' advised Frankie. 'If you did do it, I'd go and hide up somewhere and hope she don't die.'

'Fuck off! You don't think I did it, do you?' Was he winding me up, or did he mean it?

'What you do is your business. We all lose it sometimes when we do too many pills.' He glanced at Mo, silently telling me that she'd already told him about me at Black Rock and had therefore probably told the Old Bill the same thing. As far as they could see, I was therefore a crazed drug fiend who needed to be arrested very quickly indeed.

No, no, no . . . they couldn't pin it on me just because

I knew Dinger, surely not. The trouble was, I didn't believe for a moment that Dinger was capable of harming a hair on Lil's head either. And if he had an alibi, where did that leave me if anything happened to Lil?

Frankie was spot on with his advice, of course, but I had no faith in the police; they'd stitch me up if they could get away with it unless I could convince them I really didn't do it. What a fucking risk.

But I couldn't run from something I didn't do.

I downed my tea and stood up. 'I'd better go and see them then,' I said. Now I recognised the foreboding feeling I'd had earlier – it was a feeling that something, somewhere, was badly wrong.

At the crowded police station I was shown by the Desk Sergeant into a little room and told to sit down and wait.

After about half an hour, bored with studying the frosted small-pane windows, the parquet flooring, the light-oak green-rexine-covered chairs and the cream paintwork, I tried the door handle but found I was locked in. And another door leading somewhere else was also locked. The bastards had me. It was only then that I realised I hadn't checked my pockets for pills, having been so preoccupied with the problem of Lil. Quickly I went through every pocket, but I was clean; I'd been thorough that night with Mo, and really had taken every last one.

It seemed years ago that we were standing in the phone box washing down dexies with bottles of Coke. That wonderful night when it was all promise and beginning, before the speed had warped a dream and turned it into a nightmare.

I hammered on both doors in turn, and eventually the Desk Sergeant came back.

'How long have I got to wait here?' I demanded to know.

'As long as it takes, sonny,' he replied, eyeing me up and down, looking for a fight.

'Look, I've got to get back to London some time today. I've just come in as a good citizen so that you can get on with your enquiries. Can't you get someone to take a statement?'

'All in good time. Just take a seat and behave yourself,' he said, moving as if to leave.

But panic gripped me then, and I tried to rush past him out of the door. I didn't trust these bastards; I shouldn't have come here in the first place. A big hand clamped itself around my face and I was hurled back into the room. He loomed before me. 'Try that again and you'll go in the cells, sonny. Don't think you can bring your London manners down here and get away with it, because you can't.'

'Listen, you fat cunt,' I shouted, beginning to lose my rag, 'I came here to help – well I've changed my mind. I want to go. Right now, okay?'

'And I'm arresting you for assaulting a police officer,' he said, leaving the room.

I waited for him to return with back-up, but instead the door opened and a plain-clothes bloke came in and told me to follow him. We went through a corridor into a larger room where half a dozen people were working, then through into an interview room somewhere in the heart of the building. Inside was a light-oak wooden desk and some hard chairs. I sat down.

He introduced himself as DC Philips, then another one came in with notepads and the pair of them sat and faced me.

'This is my colleague, DC Duncan,' said Philips. 'Start from the beginning and tell us about Lillian Phelps.'

That's a funny name, I thought. Phelps. 'Is that her name? I only know her as Lil. Look, I've been told that you want to talk to me because she's been done over, so I've come in. What do you want to know?'

'Who told you we wanted to see you?' asked Duncan.

'A mate.'

'Name?'

'I don't know his name.'

'You don't know your friend's name?'

'No . . . John.'

Philips spoke. 'Look, we're not getting off to a good start here, are we? You've come in to help us with our enquiries and the first thing, no, the second thing you tell us is a lie. Is this the way it's going to continue?'

'It doesn't matter what his name is, does it? What does matter is that you eliminate me from your enquiries,' I said, using Frankie's expression.

'Where were you this morning between midnight and one o'clock?' asked Duncan.

'Somewhere between the Pavilion and the station – I don't know the street names.'

'Doing what?'

'I'd gone up there to see a girlfriend but she'd already gone home to London. They'd had a party, a blues party, in a church hall. They're West Indians.'

'A black girl?'

'Yeah.'

'You mix with blacks, do you?'

'Why not?'

'We ask the questions. Do you mix with blacks?'

'I don't see what this has got to do with anything, but yeah, if it's important to you, I do.'

'And then what?'

'As I said, she'd already gone, so I started walking back, felt tired and got in a car to sleep.'

'Just like that?'

'Yeah.'

'Whose car?'

'How should I know?'

Duncan glared at me. 'So you've got nobody who can vouch for where you were last night.'

I knew this was going to happen. Why was I stupid enough to listen to Frankie? 'Look, I'm telling you the truth. I wouldn't have come here if I'd done anything, would I?'

'Have you got any idea what's happened to your friend Dinger?' asked Philips suddenly.

'No. The last time I saw him he was with Lil at the beach party by the Aquarium – they wandered off together.'

'In what direction?' asked Duncan.

'Towards West Pier.'

'You were watching them?'

'No. It was just the direction they went when they left.'

'But Palace Pier's before that – why not say "towards Palace Pier"?'

'Well, Palace Pier's right there. It'd be like saying "in the direction of my left foot" or something like that.'

'Did they go under Palace Pier or along the top?'

'I don't know.'

'Do you take drugs?' asked Philips suddenly.

'No.'

'Were you up at Black Rock on Saturday night?'

Fucking Mo. She's grassed me up. There was no point in denying it. 'Yeah, what's that got to do with it?'

'What did you do there?'

'Slept in someone's tent.'

'Whose tent?'

'Don't know. I was too pissed to tell.'

'Where had you been drinking?'

'On the beach.'

'Who with?'

'Some people I'd just met. They had a lot of booze. I don't see what this has got to do with last night.'

Duncan stared hard at me. 'We have information from several sources that you are an unpleasant and violent person who loses control when he takes drugs. We also have information that you left the beach party last night at approximately 12.30 and ran off up the ramp and along the promenade towards West Pier.' He paused to take a breath. 'How well do you know Lil?'

'I've seen her about a lot. She comes from the same area as me, although exactly where I don't know.'

'Are you jealous of her . . . close relationship with your friend Dinger?'

'Jealous? You must be joking.' I laughed. 'She's not really my type.'

'You're not jealous he's fucking her then?'

Cunt's trying to get me going. Good. That means he's losing it. 'He's welcome to her,' I smiled.

'You'd rather fuck blacks . . .'

Wow. Dirty bastard. That was below the belt. 'Dunno. I've never fucked one.'

'What sort of car was it?' asked Philips, changing the subject with a frown. He doesn't like Duncan, that's for sure.

'A green Cresta.'

'Registration?'

I laughed. 'I didn't have a torch and notepad on me, otherwise I'd have written it down.'

'Don't be a cheeky little cunt,' snarled Duncan.

'After you got into the green Cresta,' continued Philips, 'what did you do then?'

'Went to sleep.'

'Just like that?'

'I was knackered.'

'Show us your hands,' said Duncan suddenly.

I held them out and they looked closely at both of them, especially the knuckles.

'Why were you "knackered", as you put it?' asked Philips.

'I don't know, I just was. I'd been dancing all night, then I'd run back down to the beach, then back up again looking for my friend. When I couldn't find her I decided to kip in a car.'

'And, of course, you were out of your mind all night the night before – on drugs.'

'I told you – I don't take drugs.'

'But you sell them. You say you don't take them, but you sell them.'

Shit. This was a new angle. How would they know that? It had to be the local girls. Yes! The local girls I'd sold pills to on the seafront on Saturday night. Also, these two cunts must know about the raid on the church hall, when I was searched and found to be clean. 'I told you, I don't take them. And I don't sell them either. I think your information's a bit dodgy. By the way, you lot searched me last night at the church hall – check with your mates. Someone must be trying to stitch me up.'

'Why would anyone want to do that?' asked Philips.

'Because he's a nasty piece of work,' answered Duncan.

Here we go. I was 'nasty' again.

There was a brief silence as both of them stared hard at me. Then Philips spoke. 'Okay, if you didn't do it, who did?'

'Haven't got a clue,' I said.

'How about your mate Dinger – he was with her, after all.'

'No way. He's hard when it comes to a fight, but with

girls? No chance.' It was true. I'd already thought about it, considered the possibility that he might have done it, but I couldn't see it. And where was he? I'd hardly given his welfare a thought until that point.

'So if you didn't do it, and he didn't do it, who did?'

'Well how the fuck should I know?'

Suddenly Philips was dead earnest. 'Look, this girl's in a bad way – she may not recover. Use your imagination, because without another line of enquiry, you're top of the list.'

Top of the list? I thought Dinger was . . .

'All right, who'd want to beat up Lil?' I said. 'Count me out. Count Dinger out. Count out all my mates.'

'Give us all the names you count out,' said Duncan.

'No way. As I was saying, who else?' I thought through the possibilities as they sat and watched me: someone with a grudge, something personal, maybe – or a random nutter. But why hadn't Dinger protected her? Or . . . yes . . . it had to be Rockers! Maybe there had still been some hanging around. 'Rockers,' I said.

'Rockers? Motorbike boys?' Philips looked as if he'd had a revelation.

'Either that or some lunatic. But as I said, Dinger can look after himself – he would have protected Lil. There'd have to have been more than one.'

Again, they both sat and stared at me.

'Do you want a cup of tea?' asked Duncan suddenly, as if he'd given up on me.

'Yes please.'

He got up and left the room.

Philips sat staring at me, then asked if Dinger was a good friend. I told him how we'd been friends at school and generally went around together.

'Do you know his family well?' he asked.

'Most of them.'

Then he asked about Lil again and why she was nick-named 'Lil the Pill' – to which I said I didn't really know, because she rarely took pills. Then he asked about Rockers again and why Mods and Rockers didn't get on, and I tried to explain that they'd been bullies for too long and had it coming to them. He seemed to understand.

Duncan brought a tray of teas in and put them on the table, then he sat down, took a packet of Player's cigarettes from his pocket and offered me one.

I took one and thanked him, thinking to myself that I'd heard all about this treatment, the hard and the soft treatment, when they tried to break you down. He gave me a light.

'Tommy,' he said suddenly, staring me in the eye, 'we have some bad news, I'm afraid.'

Oh no, I thought, Lil's died. Beyond Dinger, my last witness. Now they'll have to keep me inside longer.

'Yes . . .?' I said.

'Your friend Dinger was found earlier today. His body was washed up on the beach five hundred yards west of West Pier.'

By the time I was released it was early evening and everyone had gone home, leaving Brighton a forlorn, litter-strewn seaside town. The sun going down added a gloomy and unreal tone to the deserted gathering-places all along the front, and what had been a rare and passionate weekend was now but a ghost haunting my mind.

From one end to the other, I searched for a familiar face, someone to talk to, but not a soul could I find to help lift the burden of loneliness that had descended, and reluctantly I began the uphill walk back towards the station, knowing that I was leaving behind forever someone who'd been a major part of my life.

A hundred yards from the station, a car that I recog-nised, a maroon Jag, swerved to a stop beside me. It was Vince.

He leaned over and opened the passenger door. 'Get in,' he said, looking pale and dark-eyed.

I jumped in.

And despite everything, he managed to smile warmly when he looked at me. 'You all right son?' he asked.

'I'm all right.' I must have looked miserable, but if the truth be known I felt very little, maybe even secretly just a bit excited about it all. Other people's tragedies rarely affected me, and as far as Dinger went, all it meant was that I'd have to find someone to fill the gap he'd left. There was, of course, the interesting aspect of who might have done it – the police said that it looked like accidental death, which was bollocks – and how Vince might go about finding them, but as far as I felt, beyond being a powerful subject of conversation, it was just the end of another chapter.

Vince squeezed my shoulder, then steered the car away from the kerb.

For several miles we skirted the issue and talked about everything except Dinger, but finally he could no longer help but bring up the subject. 'You got any clues about what went on?' he asked, speeding up to overtake a posse of half a dozen scooters. I looked through the back window to see if I recognised any of them.

'The last time I saw him was around midnight on the beach by the Aquarium.'

'What was he doing?'

'He was walking away from the beach party with Lil.'

'Was he happy, you know what I mean, his usual self? Had he had any rucks with anyone?'

'If anything he seemed more . . . er . . .' I didn't know how to get it across that he seemed keen to get Lil on her own, now that he was dead. 'Well, him and Lil seemed to be getting on fine.'

Vince didn't reply for a bit. Then he said that he couldn't accept the police version of things. 'They seem to think that Dinger and Lil probably had a row; he beat her up then somehow managed to drown himself.'

I agreed it was rubbish. 'Anyway, when Lil comes out of her coma, she'll be able to tell what happened.'

'I just hope so,' said Vince. 'I just hope so. What do you reckon happened?'

'The Old Bill asked me the same thing . . .'

'They saw you?'

'Most of us.'

'Yeah, what was you saying?'

'When they asked me, I said it either had to be a nutter or Rockers, but Dinger could look after himself, so I reckon it would've needed more than one.'

'Rockers . . .' He thought about it. 'Anyone you know?'

'As far as I know, most of them had gone home after the hidings they had, but I suppose it could have been any of them.'

Outside, black-and-white cows with long shadows were chewing grass in a big flat field.

'Well, we'll just have to find 'em,' he said suddenly.

I glanced across at him and saw a vicious bastard staring back. 'If you hear anything at all, let Vince know, all right son?'

SEVEN

THE SCUFFLE OF HASTINGS

'Right, Tommy, glove up and come in here. Let's see what you can do.' It was Jack Thorne speaking, the trainer at the boxing club, an ex-pro who loved trying to keep wayward kids on the straight and narrow, as all good boxing trainers do.

I pulled the big gloves on and he laced them before sticking a pair on himself.

'Right,' he said, putting his gloves up and tapping me lightly on the chin. 'Hit me as hard as you can.'

And there it began. I missed, of course, and when I did connect it didn't seem to bother him, but from that first workout to my first public fight, he taught me to punch correctly, and in combination. I also became extremely fit.

Monday night, Tuesday night, Wednesday afternoon, Thursday night and sometimes Saturday morning, if I hadn't been out the night before, I punished my mind and body with hard, toning exercises; I skipped, worked out with the medicine ball and heavy bag, sparred, used the speed ball, ran around the streets of London for miles – backwards, forwards, sideways, shadow-boxing in front of thousands of passers-by, until Jack thought I was ready. I'd certainly never felt so fit before. Living on a diet of rare steak and salad, I felt ready to tear anyone's head from their shoulders.

The first fight, in Mile End, I won with a first-round stoppage.

And the next one in Bermondsey was the same.

And the next . . .

And the next . . .

But more importantly I got to spar with Leroy and we became friends. He was all right – he was just young and confused like all of us, and I'm not being clever here, because it was him that said it one night when we were going home together on the tube.

And Sherri was back in the frame. Neville had paved the way by telling her she was being too hard on me, that I was under no obligation to her when we were in Brighton, and that either of us was free to go out with who we wanted. So we tried again, but it wasn't easy. In fact it didn't work out at all.

The problem was really that we were so different. At first it had added to the attraction – to me she was exotic and exciting – but the reality was that she was, underneath it all, a good old-fashioned girl – the type I'd spent half my life trying to get away from. Her body was out of bounds, but she kissed like a whore – she was, in short, a prick-teaser, and I lost interest.

And there were always the social problems: for a start, neither of us would take the other one home because we feared the reaction of our parents – it had been a standing joke in my house about bringing a black girl home, so I suppose it must have been the same in hers. And when we went out together, not an evening would go by without some sort of confrontation with either blacks or whites who for some reason took offence at a black girl going out with a white boy, and it began to get on our nerves. At a blues party in Brixton I was attacked with a knife by a drunken black man who hated whites. And although he was disarmed and battered by the black doorman, I was becoming just too aware of the racial animosity on both sides of the fence and I really didn't want to be bothered with it.

But it wasn't all wasted because, as I said, I became fit, really fit, and learned how to fight.

And another strange thing happened, which I don't really know how to explain.

During the first weeks of training, Jack kept telling me I wasn't punching properly. 'No, no, no,' he'd say time and time again. 'Put power into it – you're not connecting properly.' And, to be honest, I didn't know what he was talking about – I thought I was punching good and hard; I certainly rocked some of my sparring partners. But one night, after everyone had packed up and gone, he put me to work on the heavy bag as he stood to one side watching. For an hour or more, I threw punch after punch as he adjusted my position and stance, trying to show me how the power to strike came from the ground that I stood on, until suddenly, with almost minimal effort and a combination of perfect timing and right movement, I hit the bag with such explosive force that an incredible surge of energy ran right back along my arm and hit me dead centre, sending shock-waves to my brain.

At that moment, in that split second, all my personal bricks seemed to fall into place. I suddenly realised who I was and what I was capable of. And, as if blinkers had been removed, I was able to see for the first time life itself, all around me. It was as though a wall had been knocked down, an invisible barrier between me and the rest of the universe.

A couple of days after the first match, Vince reappeared on the scene when he turned up unexpectedly at the gym. I'd told him he could find me there if he needed to talk about anything and I felt good when he walked through the door, looking confident and hard. Jack seemed to recognise him, but I had the feeling he didn't want to extend his welcome beyond the bare minimum acceptable. I finished my routine at the sound of the three-minute bell, showered and changed, and went out with Vince for a beer in the Ship.

There he told me that Lil had come out of her coma some time ago and had confirmed that she and Dinger had been attacked by a gang of Rockers. The trouble was that she was unable to identify any of the gang beyond being able to say that they were both male and female, and Vince asked if I could talk to her to see if there was the smallest clue to be dragged out which might put the finger on someone. Naturally I agreed.

We set off for Brighton in his Jag the next day, a bright Thursday morning, accompanied by two of his dodgy mates I could tell weren't bank clerks.

Lil was alone when I saw her, in a single room with a nice view into the flower gardens, but even after a month her face was still almost unrecognisable and she must have noticed the shock on my face as I tried to peer through the injuries.

'It's okay, it's me, Lil – you've got the right room,' she said, trying to smile.

I didn't know what to say. She'd never been a beauty in the traditional sense, more a character than a model out of *Vogue*, but it wasn't the time to joke about it.

She thought differently. 'I suppose anything's an improvement, though. Should thank God for small mercies. What's happening then? Who's going out with who? Where's it all happening next time? Come on, I've been starved of news lying here wrapped up like the invisible woman.'

I told her about the boxing, and Sherri, and all the newspaper reports of the riots which had included some pretty good photographs, and other news from the clubs and the West End.

'Where's it all happening next time?' she asked again.

'Seems to be happening all over the place now: Brighton, Margate, Hastings, Great Yarmouth, but I think Hastings'll be the place to be if you want to get into the papers. The Old Bill there are getting ready for it, apparently; they're going to use new control tactics for all the world to see – it'll be interesting to see what they are.'

'What d'you mean?'

'They reckon they've worked out how to knock it on the head.' I blushed when I realised what I'd said, but she didn't seem to notice.

'Tanks and machine guns, I suppose.'

I laughed, wondering how to broach the subject of her and Dinger. Vince had said that anything I found out had to be 'kept in the family', and that I wasn't to mention to her or anyone that he'd brought me down to see her.

'Lil,' I said, looking down as if I was pained, 'you know me and Dinger were best mates . . .'

She looked on silently.

'. . . well, try and remember anything you can about that night. I owe it to him.' Quickly I added, 'And you.'

'I've been over it time and again with the police, Tommy. I really don't want to go through it all again.'

'Please, Lil,' I begged.

She groaned and sagged back into the pillow. 'After we left the beach party we went for a walk along the beach, past West Pier, until we came to a bit where there weren't any other people. Dinger wanted to go and, well, sit down by the breakwater. We'd been there half an hour or so, I don't know, when a bunch of Rockers and their birds turned up.' She stopped.

'Yeah? Then what?' I asked.

'The blokes got hold of Dinger and dragged him down to the water while the girls held me.'

'Didn't he fight back?'

'What, four against one? He tried but they were too strong.'

'What about the girls?'

'What about them?' Her voice was beginning to get a bit shaky.

'They were just holding you? Didn't you shout or scream for help?'

'Course I did. But one of them hit me in the face with a stone and threatened to kill me.' She gasped, trying to hold back the tears.

'So what happened to Dinger?'

She began crying, softly at first, then more loudly until she was wailing. Quickly I grabbed her hand and cuddled her – mainly to muffle the noise in case the nurses heard and came in – and soon she quietened down. 'Don't worry,' I whispered, feeling like a fraud, 'we're going to find out who did it and sort it out. Just remember what you can.'

Bless her, she did try hard. Voice still trembling, she continued, 'They punched him about a bit, just for the fun of it, then one of them – there was one who seemed to be the leader, the one who was doing all the talking – said something about giving him a wash because he was a dirty caveman.' Despite herself, Lil laughed. 'Caveman, I ask you. Then Dinger started shouting, "You cunts, you cunts," and . . .' Battling to control herself, she stopped in mid-sentence.

'And they drowned him,' I finished for her.

'Yes,' she whispered. 'The worst thing was when . . .' She began crying again.

I waited for a bit before speaking. 'The worst thing was what?'

'When they pushed him under . . . and it all went silent.' She paused for a bit, holding on to her tears. 'It was so silent. Then one of them said, "Okay, that'll do," and they left him. Then the girls laid into me with rocks and I blacked out.'

'Fucking stroll on.' I couldn't think of anything else to say.

But I needed hard information for Vince, something he could chew over. Without that the visit would have been a waste of time. 'That's all you can remember?' I asked. 'No faces or names? Tattoos? Scars? Anything.'

'That's all.'

'He called Dinger a caveman. That's weird. They're the fucking cavemen.'

'Rocker language, I suppose. But I did have the feeling he knew Dinger.'

'What makes you say that?' I asked.

'Oh, I don't know. He struck a match and seemed to take a long look at Dinger's face. But maybe I'm imagining things. I can't think straight any more. I need to sleep, sorry Tom.'

And that was the end of it. Lil never discussed it again and the police would later say Dinger's death was 'accidental'.

Back in the car, I passed my version of the conversation with Lil to Vince, and he and his two pals seemed to think that the word 'caveman' was highly relevant. They were clutching at straws, if you ask me, but I couldn't say that.

'Don't you think it could just be the way they talk?' I asked. 'And the Beatles used to be called the Cavemen, didn't they? A lot of people think Mods dress like the Beatles.'

Vince was adamant. 'Listen, this was personal. And

"caveman" is the key. I can't see the Beatles angle at all. If anything they would have called him a Mod.'

'Personal'. I thought Vince was getting a bit carried away about the whole thing; he just wanted revenge, and saying it was personal would just make him feel better about damaging someone. Not that he needed to feel better about it. I had the feeling that if it came to it, anyone would do.

But then it dawned on me and my stomach turned over. 'Yeah!' I said. Of course. How could I be so slow? It wasn't exactly personal – at least, it didn't start out as personal – but when whoever it was struck the match and saw Dinger's face, he recognised him from somewhere. 'The caves! Chislehurst Caves!'

'What about them?'

'We used to go there some Saturday nights to listen to the bands. The last time we went we had a ruck with the bikers, and some of them got hurt. It could be any of them. But one of them – Kenser Donnelly – got stabbed, and I'm sure I saw him at the seafront on his bike.'

Vince was staring intently at me. 'Kenser Donnelly?' he repeated carefully.

'Yeah.'

'Where can I find him?'

'I don't know. Someone up the Fifty-Nine Club might know.'

'Or Johnson's,' said one of Vince's mates. 'We'll find him.'

'Fucking hooray,' spat Vince, starting the car and whacking it into gear. 'Now we're getting somewhere!'

He drove back to London at speed and dropped me off at the Roaring Twenties. As I jumped out of the car he promised to keep me informed about Kenser Donnelly, and added that I might be needed later when they caught up with him.

I had to say that I thought the evidence was a bit thin. Dinger had punched a few faces that night in the caves, but I was the one who'd punched Kenser.

'But at least we've got somewhere to start,' said Vince. 'And believe you me, son, we'll find out very quickly if it was him or not. And if it wasn't, he'll soon start pointing fingers in the right direction – they all do.'

The way he said 'they all do' sounded well naughty; it meant that he was used to this line of business, used to making people talk whether they wanted to or not.

But who were these people? As I've said, I knew that Vince and his mates were villains, and I was forming my own ideas of what a villain should be, but it was beginning to look as if my views were based on little other than comic-book romance and ignorance, you know the sort of thing: tough good guys, rough diamonds and all that shit. They'd done nothing outrageous that could have made me feel this way, but the grim nonchalance with which they'd approached the whole issue of Dinger was a disturbing revelation. Glamour didn't come into it.

By the time the August bank holiday came around again, Vince and co. were but a distant memory to me. Dinger was a diminishing void in my life, his position as my closest friend having been taken up by Frankie, and Mac was well on the way to being married, having found himself a tasty little sort whose parents were loaded. Now it was me, Frankie, Jacko, Alan and Micky who were hanging out together; a natural progression away from old schoolfriends.

Frankie was still sending Norma out to work, although he couldn't see it lasting much longer because she was getting more independent, Jacko was a burglar and gambler, Micky worked in the stock exchange and Alan was a lighterman. I, because of family and financial pressures, had taken a job as a trainee with an electric company and was now the lowest-paid of all. Worse still, I had no time free to continue the lifestyle I'd been used to and had to resort to taking part in fiddles at work, like claiming for unworked hours, to earn extra money. Everyone fiddled their hours like this, and although it was still thieving – being paid for work you never did – nobody saw it in that light and preferred to regard it as a perk of the job. Millions of pounds must have been lost every year in that way.

I only mention it because while this is going on big time all over the place and everyone turns a blind eye, as soon as one of us kids as much as swipes a packet of fags we're dragged off down the nick and subjected to various crude brainwashing techniques.

But my parents were temporarily appeased, and as long as they were happy, well, what more could I say? To them it meant that for forty hours a week it was guaranteed I'd be out of the way.

What is it with this fucking work thing anyway? They'd had to live through hard times and a depression and terrible poverty and running around with no shoes on their feet and four of them sharing a bed and bed bugs running up the wall and the old man coming home drunk and there being no food on the table – and I'm sure it was terrible – but they still went around bowing and scraping to those who were the cause of all the problems. And they were *still* doing it. As far as I could see, they were all brainwashed. As soon as we said, 'Hold on a minute, I don't want any of this misery,' they called us anti-social and sided with the sly fuckers who were having us over.

If only they could have said, 'Good on you, try and do what we, your parents, failed so miserably to do – stand up against them.'

But they didn't. They betrayed us.

I had to get out, there was no way around it. The only trouble was that my wages were so poor I couldn't afford a flat, and all the time I was at home I couldn't save money because I couldn't bear to stay in the house, so I went out and spent it.

The old man didn't want me about the house, but when I came in he went on about me going out. If I stayed in, my mother would lend me money to go out, to avoid having to look at my 'long face', as she called it, and the following week, of course, when I had to pay back the money, the situation became worse and I had to borrow more money to get out again.

To make things worse, this was all going on at a time of my life when sex came second only to breathing. Where could I take girlfriends? Groping on doorsteps, or on trains, or in the park, or in dark corridors or someone else's bed at parties was no longer cool; after all, I was nearly nineteen and becoming sophisticated. Just two weeks earlier, while mother and father were away, I'd brought a girl home from Peckham Discothèque and we'd 'made love', as they say, in my own bed – an amazing experience impaired only by the girl calling me a 'fucking cunt' for coming after about ten seconds without wearing a johnny.

But these things would change. All I needed was more space to myself and more practice, and I planned to get it.

Despite what all the social experts and commentators said, the driving force behind us was always sex. Clothes were worn that would appeal to members of the opposite sex; our lifestyle was conducted in a way thought to be attractive to the opposite sex; and we always went where the opposite sex was – despite the amphetamines, which didn't put you off but just made the act practically impossible for males. The few geezers I came across who tried to put it across that they weren't obsessed by sex – as some of the reports which were coming out were trying to suggest – were either sly bastards pretending to be cool, mentally ill or queer.

As I've said, swallowing dozens of amphetamine pills did little to improve your reputation as a great lover, and it was probably this that caused such a swift turnover in relationships. The only girls who went out with pill-heads for longer than one or two nights were usually confirmed virgins, and that only lasted until the speeding stopped and the erections started, when they'd do a runner.

Slowly, alcohol played a greater and greater part in all of our lives as the image of the Mod as an under-age pill-popper became unpalatable. Fighting was seen more and more as a way of life rather than as a reaction to the presence of Rockers, and Mods began to look to other Mods when they couldn't find anyone else to fight.

Hastings, far from being the high point of the so-called Mod movement, was the death of it. August 1964.

Compared with Brighton, the atmosphere at Hastings – a second-rate watering hole for all the south London misfits – was less exuberant, less powerful, altogether more diluted by the pale hordes who'd come to jump on the Mod bandwagon on the off chance that they might get seen on television or get their photographs in the papers and there-fore be able to claim a part in what they saw as the glory of youth rebellion. And when it came to Old Bill crunch time, it was clear that the spirit of Brighton and Margate was missing when everyone allowed themselves to be rounded up and herded out of town.

As for me, I spent the whole weekend in Hastings with a beautiful little sort who drove me mad with lust but wouldn't let me touch her because, she said, she was engaged and didn't want to be unfaithful to her boyfriend. Ah.

And another young Mod boy was found drowned, exactly like Dinger. According to the police, it too was an accident.

But the papers were jubilant. According to them, five thousand footsore teenage invaders had a lousy weekend after being marched from one end of the town to the other by local police reinforced by two plane-loads of volunteers from London. Copying the Grand Old Duke of York's strategy, they marched them up to the top of the hill and marched them down again. The youngsters were shifted along like sheep and herded out of town, the police like sheepdogs guarding their flock and rounding up any strays.

Arrests totalled seventy-four, but damage was negligible.

The local Top Man in the force said it was a purely spontaneous piece of good policemanship. And about the dead boy he said they had 'an open mind'.

So, a nice bit of propaganda there for the masses. Despite it being almost totally incorrect yet again. Now the frightened public could sleep easily in their beds instead of worrying about teenagers on the rampage. Good old police. Good old Bobbies. Makes you proud to be fucking English, don't it?

I saw the same bloke getting arrested in three different parts of town, every time conveniently near a photographer. None of us knew him, and the way he was dressed up was unbelievable, like a refugee from a jumble sale, someone's strange idea of how a young troublemaker should look. A police cadet or an out-of-work actor stooging for the cameras.

And then we had a modern version of Judge Jeffreys going over the top and putting people inside for minor infringements of the law – in direct contrast to the news and police reports of the situation being under control. Over half of the thirty-two kids who admitted taking part in the weekend 'Battle of Hastings' were sent to detention centres. And three young men were jailed.

Before sentencing them, the chairman of Hastings magistrates said, 'This is a deliberately cultivated form of modern wickedness. There is no reason for this so-called hatred between Mods and Rockers – it is merely an excuse for excitement, thieving and violence.'

He said that Hastings had suffered for three days and nights in an appalling atmosphere of tension and apprehension, sometimes mounting to terror. 'This was caused by an invasion of mindless adolescent morons, who came here deliberately to make trouble in the hope that they would cause as much noise, damage and distress as possible, and to escape the consequences. We must take into account the overall effect on the thousands of citizens, and on the visitors to the borough.'

It was time for parliament to consider what measures it should take to crush 'this form of mass hooliganism, which is apparently repetitive at holiday time', he added. He obviously hadn't read the reports of good policemanship and the ease with which the crowd had been controlled. 'If nothing is done,' he continued, 'thousands of innocent people will continue to suffer injury, fear and damage to property.'

Only thousands? Why not millions? As far as I could see, the only danger to society was him.

Out of twenty-one kids who pleaded guilty to charges ranging from assaulting the police to threatening behaviour, ten were sentenced to three months in a detention centre, two were sent for three months and fined £50 with an alternative of an extra three months' detention, three were fined £25 and one was fined £10. One was sent for six months' detention, another for two terms of three months' detention each. One kid was given four months, another three months with a fine of £25 or an extra three months, and a 'man' of twenty-one was given two months, yes, two months, for breaking a car headlamp.

All of them were bound over for £25 to keep the peace for two years. Two years! Just so much as glance at one of the Old Bill from then on and you're inside straight away for breach of the peace.

Police carried a pile of sheath knives and studded leather belts into the courtroom before proceedings started just to put Judge Jeffreys and the press in the right mood, and the accused kids were all paraded before them, handcuffed together in pairs.

What a way to treat kids who were trying to clean up society.

Two days later, my luck changed and my life veered off in another direction. Vince called and asked if I wanted a job as a messenger and general help, cash in hand, offering three times what I was earning, plus bonuses, which he said were good; so I arranged to meet him in a café in Berwick Street the following morning.

'No, no, it's nothing to do with the stall – you don't want to sell fruit and veg, do you?' Vince was setting my mind at rest about what he wanted me to do.

'I wasn't sure,' I said. 'I don't mind stall work – it's just the early mornings. I don't think I'd be reliable.'

Vince looked hard at me. 'You're going to have to be reliable,' he said. 'Be around whenever we need you, although generally speaking you'll be working afternoons and evenings up here.' He took a sip of his tea and a shadow passed over his face. 'I was going to train Dinger into it, but he didn't have the head on his shoulders, God bless him. He was too impetuous – couldn't see a situation where a bit of decorum was needed, know what I mean?'

I laughed, but couldn't see any mileage in agreeing with him. 'What exactly is it you want me to do?' I asked.

'Basically it's rent collecting and personal deliveries with a bit of escort work thrown in – you'll like that – but you'll have to get yourself suited up. Have you got one?'

'I've got four decent suits.'

He put his hand in his pocket, 'Don't use them, save 'em for best. Here, go along to Paul's and get measured up.' And he handed me a hundred notes. 'Oh, by the way,' he added, 'we caught up with a Ray Matthews and a Fred Belotti . . .' He scrutinised my face for signs of recognition.

'Never heard of them,' I said.

'Mates of your Kenser Donnelly. Anyway, they put the finger on him.'

'What do you mean?'

'What I mean is, they owned up to being there, but he's the main man we're looking for.'

'You got any idea where he is?'

'When we caught up with Matthews and Belotti he did a moonlight to the States, but he'll be back.'

'Can't you get Interpol on to him?' I stupidly asked.

Vince almost choked on his bacon roll. 'He's got no case to answer. They're still saying it was accidental death, which suits me. Just like Matthews and Belotti.' He sipped his tea and allowed me to take in what he was saying.

So Matthews and Belotti were dead. Accidentally.

'That leaves three,' he continued. 'Donnelly, Franklin and Waterson. There were three birds involved as well, but they were the ones who gave this Lil of yours a good hiding. I've told her family who they are, now it's up to them.'

'Franklin and Waterson being two more bikers?'

'Yeah, there were five of them. Four of them held him under while the fifth one kept a lookout.'

I shuddered as I visualised the scene: Dinger struggling

like crazy while being held under water. 'What are you going to do with them?' I asked, not really expecting a truthful answer.

'Come along and see,' he said. 'We question them. Get them to see the error of their ways. They turn religious and start praying. Then we send them away on a long holiday.'

Maybe I was a bit nervous, but I couldn't help laughing. Vince's sense of humour appealed to me. 'All right,' I said, 'I'll come when you catch up with Kenser Donnelly.' I added that he'd once raped a girl at our school, leaving out the fact that I'd been there and done nothing about it.

Vince nodded his head thoughtfully. 'Did he now? I do believe Dinger said something about that. He's not very nice, is he, this Donnelly character? We'll have to make sure he repents. I've got one or two friends who love people like him.'

I asked Vince when I could start work.

He looked at his watch. 'Now, if you like.'

I jumped at it, then added hopefully that I wanted to find a flat of my own.

'What's wrong with your mother and father's place?' he asked.

'They're driving me insane. All the time they're on about something or the other. Just because I don't want to wear what they want me to wear, or do the jobs they want me to do . . .'

'There's no place like home, son.'

'I mean it. They've got no room for me as I am.'

Vince swallowed his tea. 'You finished?' he asked, looking at my cup. 'I've got a nice little place just around the corner you can use if you want – it'll be coming up vacant in a day or two. Have a look at it; take it or leave it.'

Two days later, after it had been vacated and cleaned out, I moved into a little one-bedroomed flat on the top floor of a block just off Brewer Street, Soho. It had a sagging bed, a settee, a tiny bathroom and WC and an even tinier kitchen with a double gas ring and a sink. But it was perfect, with rooftop access to the rest of the block, just like Nicole's old room. My dream had come true. And the rent was going to be deducted straight from my wages.

The first job was easy: all I had to do was collect the rent from a theatrical clothes shop in Berwick Street and sit on the cash until Vince or one of his mates turned up to collect it from me. Without so much as a 'hello', the proprietor just took the money from the till, handed it to me and walked away.

After three weeks my new suit, a single-breasted midnight-blue kid mohair, was ready, and I bought a couple of pink Sea Island cotton shirts with button-down collars to go with it. I'd fancied a change from Tonik, and worn with a dark-blue knitted silk tie and complementary black basket-weave shoes I looked just about right for an aspiring Soho businessman.

Of course, it didn't take long to learn what Vince's business was all about – personal security and protection with a whole string of sidelines such as courier and escort work – and I soon became an expert 'rent collector', as they called it, taking a handy two per cent commission on everything I brought in, which enabled me to save money for the first time in my life.

Occasionally the tenants were reluctant to pay, for one reason or another, but being on commission I just did my best to look serious and kept going back until they paid up. Soon I was collecting other debts and parcels from all over London, and I got to use Vince's Jag, as soon as I'd passed the driving test, instead of having to use buses, taxis or the tube.

One day I had to take a suitcase to an address near

Sydenham in south London. The only instructions I'd had from Vince were that if for any reason I should have any problems with the police, all I had to do was say nothing but make a telephone call to a London number and I'd be released. Although I never had any cause to use this system, it made me wonder exactly what links Vince and his team had; I knew that he mixed with some of the blokes who were in the flying squad because Frankie had pointed them out, and I thought at first that perhaps he was some sort of informer, but when I asked him about his friends he just said they were useful to know but worth keeping away from, whatever that meant.

Being an inquisitive sort of person, I stopped south of Tower Bridge beneath a railway arch so that I could see if I was being followed and picked the lock to the case just to see what line of business I was dealing with this time. Inside was a carrier bag containing something wrapped in news-paper, and when I looked inside I wished I hadn't. It was someone's arms – male, tattooed arms with the tips of all the fingers missing. One of the tattoos said 'MUM'.

Carefully rewrapping the parcel so that no one could see it had been tampered with, I put it back in the suitcase, locked it again and continued with the journey. Not being particularly squeamish, I soon recovered, but the discovery had caught me by surprise and I drove all the way to Sydenham without remembering one bit of the journey.

Another job I had to do after passing my test was to go and pick up a young woman from an address off the Old Kent Road and taxi her about, usually to West End hotels. Sometimes I waited and sometimes I didn't but she always gave me plenty of money to pass on to Vince. She called herself Monica, spoke with a plum in her mouth and, apart from being fabulous to look at, in the style of Liz Taylor's Cleopatra, had the most amazing pointed tits I'd ever seen.

Confident in that I now had nearly four hundred pounds saved, one night I plucked up the courage to ask if she'd consider me as a client, but she dismissed the idea out of hand, saying that I was too young, and that anyway, her clients were rich and sophisticated.

'But I'll pay, just like they do,' I insisted.

'It's not the point, darling,' she said, looking down her lovely nose at me as she reapplied her lipstick. 'I must keep up appearances. I can't be seen socialising with spotty taxi-drivers, can I?' And she laughed. In fact, she always had that sort of amused look on her face when she spoke to me, as if she were making her mind up about something.

Stuck-up cow, I thought; just who did she think she was anyway? I didn't have any spots. Well, the occasional one or two, maybe. There would have been a time when a put-down like that would have crippled me for days or even weeks, but I was slowly beginning to feel my feet as my head got to grips with the social ways of this weird country. She was only a whore, after all.

If nothing else, Vince had taught me that money was everything and I knew there had to be a way to get my hands on those knockers, so I got to know a couple of Mod bellboys in the hotels she worked at and found out, as I had suspected, that she was freelancing on the days she was supposed to be taking off.

On the way home one night a couple of weeks later, I confronted her with it and, fearing that her freelancing might have already been agreed with Vince, I was relieved when she reacted as I'd hoped. 'How dare you spy on me!' she gasped. 'If you're not careful I'll get someone to come and have a little chat with you.' It looked better by the minute. Now she was threatening me.

'Listen, Nicky,' I said. She hated being called Nicky. 'If anyone's going to be doing any chatting, it's me. And remember the way unfaithful toms get treated. Arctic Rose never did look the same after that razor job. Imagine having to go back to work in a factory with one half of your face an inch lower than the other.' I was learning how to threaten people as well – it came in useful for rent collecting.

There was a long silence as she stared out of the window, then she lit a cigarette. 'Okay,' she said finally, 'how much do you want?'

I smiled at her through the rear-view mirror. 'I don't want money – I want time,' I said.

She stared back impatiently. 'What the hell are you talking about, "time"?'

'With you. Time with you. I offered to pay before, but you laughed, said I was too low for you, so now it'll have to be free. Or I report back about the extra income you've been keeping to yourself.'

I could see she was getting angry. 'Listen, you bastard,' she hissed, and her quizzical smirk faltered for a second. 'What I do in my spare time is up to me. We have an agreement. Now stop the car.' We had arrived at her drop-off point.

I looked at the lovely face I saw every night in my dreams. 'Sleep on it. Let me know tomorrow. I know it's your day off, but I'll pick you up at the same time anyway.'

She wrapped herself in her coat and marched away without saying goodnight. She had nice legs too. And she definitely wiggled her arse, knowing that I was watching.

That night I rang the Victoria Hotel and booked a room, then went round to see Vince and told him everything.

'You cheeky little fucker!' he said. He seemed amazed that I'd told him. But I was smarter than anyone gave me credit for. The worst that could happen would be that he'd order me not to see her again. But I'd still get a lot of credit for passing the information to him. As for her, well, Vince wasn't the striping kind; he'd no more damage a lady than hurt his own mother. Well, that's what I told myself. Vince was still almost as much a mystery to me as he was the first day I'd met him; for all I knew he could be Jack the Ripper.

And it paid off. He told me to take her under my wing as my own client – he called everyone who gave him money a 'client' – and said that providing his income increased rather than decreased he'd be more than happy.

At three the following afternoon, after a good soak in the bath and a sprinkling of Tabac aftershave, I went to pick her up and, as I'd guessed, she was there, looking as delectable as ever. In fact she looked even tastier than usual.

'Nice to see you again,' I said.

'The pleasure's all yours,' she replied without smiling, and got in the back.

For a while I let the silence work its own magic before asking her if she'd made up her mind.

'I don't have much choice, do I?'

'Great. Let's forget past differences then. D'you fancy a drink?'

But she was still cool. 'Can we just get on with it?'

'Fair enough. But don't say I didn't try.'

The hotel room was large and airy with a bathroom and lavatory to one side. The windows looked out over a wooded square where an old lady was feeding the pigeons with bread taken from her pushalong trolley.

'Here,' I said, 'let me take your coat.' I took her camel coat and hung it up as she paced about, smoking another king-size cigarette. She appeared to be preoccupied with something.

'Okay,' she said, suddenly very businesslike, stubbing out the cigarette. 'What do you want?'

Despite all the surface bravado, I was very unsure of

myself and how she might react to my approach. Holding my breath, I walked over to her, hesitated for a second, then unbuttoned her blouse and ran my hands over her breasts. 'You've got the best tits I've ever seen,' I said, my heart beginning to pound. 'I'll just play with them for a bit if that's all right with you.'

'I must hear that half a dozen times a week,' she replied coolly, staring me in the eye. 'Do you want to fuck them?'

Fuck them. That sounded like an excellent idea. 'Okay,' I said.

Nonchalantly removing her blouse and bra, she sat on the edge of the bed and cupped her hands beneath her breasts, holding them ready. I stood in front of her, dropped my strides and boxers and pushed my dick in between. Then she began to twist up and down, until suddenly I experienced such an explosion of an orgasm that my knees almost gave way. I noticed that she was watching me intently as this was happening, like a cat watching a mouse, and for a moment I thought she might be getting off on it.

'I've come all over your pearls,' I said, collapsing in an armchair, but she didn't appear too bothered about it, even managing that little smile as she disappeared into the bathroom.

After she'd cleaned up I told her to get dressed.

'Are we going back already?' she asked. She seemed a little surprised.

'No.'

'Then what's the point in getting dressed?' she asked as she slowly fastened the buttons on her blouse.

'Come here.'

She walked over and stood before me.

I ran my hand up her stockinged leg to her crutch. 'I've come. Now it's your turn.' I began rubbing her cunt.

For a few seconds she stood still, then softly said, 'It's going to take more than that.'

'Like what?' I asked.

'Fuck me.'

'No. I want to watch you come.'

'Well fuck me with your eyes open.'

'I'll be too busy coming myself.'

Those green Cleopatra eyes bored intensely into mine. The probing was getting to her.

'Can't I lie down while you're doing this?'

'No. I want you to stand there and come in front of me. Take your top off again.'

She removed her blouse and bra and I sat up and took a nipple in my mouth, watching her eyes all the time. As I rolled my tongue round and round, slowly her eyes closed and her breath came quicker and quicker, until finally she gasped and breathed out sharply as she came. Quickly I pushed her on to the bed, pulled her knickers aside and began fucking her, at first slowly, then harder and harder, until she peaked again, crying out, as I came inside her.

It was the first time I'd seen a fully grown woman come, and the most beautiful moment of my life. All I wanted to do was see it again and again and again. I looked at her beautiful, serene face and kissed her on the cheek, then buried my face in her exquisite, perfumed neck.

I remembered the schoolboy sacrifice of Marilyn Wisheart then, her agonised face as Kenser Donnelly raped her, and felt the deep, hidden pain of that far-off encounter surfacing, freed by the sight of Monica's passion. I suddenly felt inexplicably choked and began to cry silently, as a cocktail of emotions tore me apart.

A manicured hand ran through my hair. 'Why are you crying?' she asked softly.

I couldn't tell her about Marilyn Wisheart or the release

I'd felt by watching her come because I didn't understand it myself, but I apologised for holding her to ransom, which I suddenly realised was little better than rape itself.

She laughed, as if amused by it all. 'I wouldn't be here if I didn't want to be here.'

'But you didn't have any choice. I blackmailed you.'

'It wouldn't have made any difference if you had told Vince. Don't you understand? I just pay him for protection from time to time, and he gives it to me. He's not my pimp, you know.'

So she knew all along that Vince wouldn't touch her. 'So why turn up today then?' I asked.

She leaned over and kissed me on the mouth. 'Because the thought of you thinking you were blackmailing me turned me on.'

I sat up. 'So you were fucking me, then?' I'd been had over.

'Could say that. Don't tell me you didn't like it.'

The following spring I took some time off and went to St Ives in Cornwall with Frankie and Jacko and Micky in a Mini-Cooper S I'd bought with my Christmas bonus.

Vince had suggested it. Monica, or my 'posh tart', as he called her, had begun taking up more and more of my time until the rent-collecting had got behind. Underneath her glamorous cover she was a very sweet girl from a well-known family who had got into debt somewhere along the line, but the snag was, I was beginning to get involved and resented her seeing other men, so I was taking a break to cool the relationship down a bit.

The caravan was on a site just outside town, and the smell inside brought back gut-churning memories of family holidays: endless rain, comics, Calor gas and pacamacs. Dumping our cases, we set off straight into town to check out the pubs with the intention of getting pissed and trying out the local talent. But we didn't realise that the local boys wouldn't take kindly to flash Londoners who came down trying to take over.

It has to be said that they could only have judged us by the way we looked because we began very quietly, being unsure of the ground, and did our best to be good citizens. But in one harbourside pub, Micky was so aggravated by the comments of one of the yokels, a loud-mouthed folk singer in sandals who kept referring to us as 'slumscum', that he decked him and got us barred, setting the stage for what was going to be a week of anything but relaxation.

Mods hadn't arrived in St Ives, and although we didn't class ourselves as Mods – Micky said we were 'Gods', not 'Mods', when asked – we were identified as belonging to that group by the few locals able to read a newspaper.

Giving things a chance to blow over, the next day we went and saw all the sights – Land's End and other unimpressive crap – and did a tour of the backwaters and hidden pubs of Cornwall which provided sanctuary for all the mutants and inbred oddities that found themselves running out of dry land to stand on. The hilarious thing was that they regarded *us* as weird, and in every pub we visited the regulars just stood about whispering and glancing through their beer glasses until we got spooked and left.

Getting bored by the third day, we turned over a jewellery shop by crowding and confusing the owner while someone else cleared the window. But that evening, over-confident and full of beer, we went to a shabby nightclub outside town called the Blue Lagoon looking for birds and blew it badly when Jacko tried to sell a stolen watch to a friendly yokel, who naturally enough crept off and told the management, who in turn called the police.

Shortly after, the management – a couple of fading Teddy boys gone respectable – came over warily to tell us that the place was surrounded and that we'd better sit quietly and await arrest. Then they crept off and locked themselves in their office.

We looked at each other. Sit quietly? They still had a lot to learn about London boys. Without thinking, I suggested the best way out would be to create a diversion by starting a riot, and the moment I put the idea forward Frankie punched me in the mouth, knocking me over backwards on to a table loaded with other people's drinks. Jacko and Micky laid into anyone within reach and within seconds the brawl had spread from one end of the club to the other. Tables and chairs were flying, women were screaming, and all the windows went in one after another.

Seizing our moment, we ran out through the main entrance, but police were swarming all over the place and we had to split up and make a dash in different directions in an attempt to escape. Wearing light-coloured clothes, I was soon picked out by torchlight, run to ground, arrested, along with Micky, and taken into police custody. Frankie and Jacko got away.

Talk about humiliation. After years of law-breaking I'd been captured in Cornwall by a bunch of yokels. What a piss-off. Not that we were in any danger; it just felt bad to be manhandled by amateurs.

Being flush, we'd only gone in the shop for the crack while the other two did the thieving, so neither of us was carrying any loot – and we also knew the score should more than one of us be pulled in at any time for questioning, which was to deny all knowledge of the crime but refuse to vouch for anyone else's good character. This confuses the issue and makes your questioner think you're telling the truth, because as soon as you start saying your mates are honest, they know you're lying – how does anyone really know what their mates have been up to?

We weren't worried at all, and to prove it to the onlooking crowd, Micky put on the policeman's helmet that was lying on the back seat of the panda car and gave them two fingers. But any pull was a little defeat and, thinking long-term, they always kept records, which had to be worse than no record at all. Don't let them tell you otherwise.

Inside the nick we were both interrogated for what remained of the evening.

'We understand that you have in your possession some stolen watches.'

'Sorry, officer, not me. You can search me if you like. Who told you that, anyway?'

'Can you turn out your pockets please?'

'Delighted to. There you are. Nothing.'

'Thank you very much.'

'Don't mention it, officer.'

'Tell me, are any of your friends in possession of stolen goods?'

'Not that I know of, but I don't really know them that well. We just came down on holiday together.'

'Are you absolutely sure?'

'Absolutely.'

'And you've never seen any stolen watches?'

'Not at all. But, as I say, I can't speak for anyone else. If there's anything I can do to help, just let me know. The last thing I need is all this, being attacked by the locals and having to run like that. I think someone was jealous because we were chatting up their birds.'

'But you've never seen any watches?'

'No, officer.'

'Do you think your friend next door might know anything about them?'

'I really don't know. As I said, I don't know him very well. What he gets up to is his business.'

'Were you together all day today?'

'Most of the day, yes.'

'Did you go into Pandora's Box this morning?'

'Pandora's Box, officer? I couldn't tell you. Is that a pub?'

'A jeweller's in the High Street.'

'Oh yes. I remember. It was quite crowded at the time, lots of old women and one or two locals I've seen about.'

'Mmm . . . You didn't see anyone take any watches?'

'Er, no – although there was a big swarthy bloke who came in, hung around the window for a few seconds, then left.'

'Can you describe him?'

'Well, big, black hair, bushy eyebrows. I'm not suggesting he took anything.'

'No, but describe him anyway.'

There followed a good description of the bumpkin who had grassed us up.

Then we went over it all in fine detail, twice more. Easy, because there were no lies to remember, except the bit about the swarthy local being in the shop.

The officer closed his book, looked at his watch, then said, 'Goodnight. Try to stay out of trouble.'

'Thank you, officer, and goodnight.'

He didn't even want any fingerprints.

The last few days I spent quietly attempting to seduce a convent virgin – who broke down in tears when I finally managed to breach her defences, albeit momentarily and after plying her with vodka, sobbing that she'd been defiled and was on the path to hell.

EIGHT

THE ORGANISATION

Back home, Vince called me up and said we had some 'teamwork' to carry out immediately over in south-east London and I didn't even get the chance to speak to Monica before two car-loads of us sped off in the direction of Lewisham, where an associate of Vince's had been having problems with a little crew who were trying to set up a string of bookies in direct competition with him. Worse, they'd used threats and some violence on his staff to intimidate them into leaving their jobs and it was felt that the time had come for a show of strength.

'There's a reason I've brought you along,' said Vince as we passed New Cross Station.

'I didn't think I was coming for the change of air,' I said, still pissed off that I'd been dragged away from Monica.

He went on. 'The lads who are causing the bother are apparently about your age, your style, you know what I mean.'

'Moddy boys,' added a muscle-bound bloke who was sitting next to me, with a sarcastic grin.

'I'm *not* a fucking Mod! They're the geezers in parkas and Fred Perrys.' Our image had been so defiled by newspapers and newcomers to the scene that outright denial was now necessary. Frankie had started labelling us as 'Smoovies' instead.

'Come on, admit it,' he teased, 'you're a Mod. I mean, if you're not a Rocker you've got to be a Mod.'

No imagination, these thugs.

Vince went on. 'You'll know their language and the way their minds work, so I want you to go in and talk to them and try to convince them either to stop what they're doing or at least to move on somewhere else. Also find out if they've got back-up. We don't think so, we think they're working on their own, but they might just be a front for someone else.'

He wanted me to go in alone. 'I hope they're not tooled up,' I said.

'What if they are? Just talk to them nicely and convince them there's no need for violence.'

'But why me? Anyone can do that.'

'We're known. I'd rather clear it up without getting the credit for this one. We couldn't trust anyone else to do it, and if it comes to it we will do it ourselves, but if you can just talk them into changing their ways, it could save a lot of grief.'

Shortly afterwards we pulled up in front of a dingy row of shops.

Vince looked at a shop that was boarded up. 'That one – the one boarded up. They're in there. Go and knock on the door. When they answer, just go in and talk to them.'

'If they agree to move out of the area, where can they operate?' I asked.

'One thing at a time. If they agree to that we'll come in and talk to them. If they don't, well, we'll have to come in anyway. So do your best.'

Stepping out of the car, I looked about, then crossed the pavement to the front door and knocked. After a couple of minutes it opened.

'Tommy!' The geezer knew me! It was Dave Smart, an old mate from school, who stood there.

'Dave! How you going?' I couldn't believe it. This would

be a piece of cake. At school he'd been lower down in the pecking order, and I couldn't see any reason for changing that. 'What are you doing here? Can I come in?'

He showed me in, through an empty shop and up some stairs to a scruffy flat above. Inside were another four blokes in Tonik suits, all about my age, and I recognised one of them, Danny, as part of the first wave at Brighton. As far as I could see they were probably all good blokes just trying to make a living. 'So what brings you here?' asked Dave. 'D'you want to put a bet on?'

I laughed. 'No. Nothing like that. Look, I'll come to the point. Take a look outside.'

They did. 'The two cars?' said someone.

'Yeah. Inside are nine very heavy geezers who are waiting to come in here and close you down.'

All eyes were on me.

'But,' I said, 'they've asked me to come in and talk to you first. If you agree to their rules, there'll be no problem.'

Dave spoke first. 'Where do you come into all this?'

'By chance. Purely by chance. I didn't know who I was coming to meet, but they needed someone of the same age, they said, to try to talk to you first.'

'Fuck off,' said Danny. 'We've been through all this before with the local heavy mob, and we saw them off. Another bunch don't worry us. We've got friends as well.'

'Believe me, they're not jokers,' I said earnestly.

Dave asked who they were.

'From the Elephant,' I lied.

'The fucking Elephant! What's Lewisham got to do with the fucking Elephant?' cried Danny, beginning to get angry.

I sympathised. 'I don't know, I'm just the messenger boy. Believe me, I've got other places I'd rather be.'

'And you say if we don't agree to their rules they'll be in here?'

'Yeah.'

Dave looked at the others, then back at me. 'What are these rules? Do you know?'

'All I know is it's something about territory. If you agree to move out of the area, no problem.'

Dave thought for a moment as the others began arguing, then asked if I'd wait downstairs while they had a discussion. He even apologised for that.

Downstairs I picked up an old *Health and Efficiency* magazine and flicked through the pages looking at the nudes. None of them had tits like my Monica. I remembered the last time we'd shagged and she'd said I'd have to start using johnnies because she didn't want to get pregnant. That made me feel sad because it meant the madness had gone.

Upstairs I could hear arguing, but eventually it fell silent and Dave came down. 'We've agreed that providing we get a good patch of our own, we'll move out,' he said.

I was genuinely pleased. I didn't want to see these geezers get hurt – they were my own kind. Telling Dave to leave the door ajar, I trotted back to the car and stuck my head through the window to talk to Vince. 'It's okay,' I said, pleased with myself. 'They'll talk areas. No problem at all.'

'How many of them?' asked Vince. It was then that I noticed they all had baseball bats.

'Five. You won't need those, though.'

'Are they tooled up?'

'No. As I say, you won't need those. They're sweet.'

Ignoring me, Vince looked at the others and they got out of the car, followed by the five from the other car, and walked briskly towards the shop. What were they doing? I'd sorted it out. A few seconds later I heard shouting and smashing and ran back into the shop to see what was going on. Inside, on the floor, lay Dave, his head smashed in. Upstairs was worse. The other four had been battered beyond recognition with the baseball bats, their suits splattered with blood, ruined.

Vince glanced at me. 'Right! All out. Time for home.'

Confused and angry, I followed and we piled back into the cars and sped away.

After a while Vince spoke. 'You might be pissed off about what just happened, but it had to be done, Tommy.'

'Yeah, but why bother to involve me at all? All I've done is made myself out to be a right cunt. They were all right, and now they'll think I was in on it.'

'I'm sure they were all right, I'm sure they were, but it's the way it is. Someone pays us to do a job and we do it, whether we like it or not.'

'You knew all along what you were going to do – but I still don't get why you had to use me.'

'I told you – we didn't know if someone else was behind them. The last thing anyone wants right now is a gang war across London; it'd just damage business. So by sending you in we could find out – and you did a grand job. If anyone else had been involved – if there had been another firm behind them – your boys wouldn't have been able to make a decision like that without speaking to their governors first – either that or they would have laughed in your face.'

I began to see the logic. But whichever way you looked at it, it was me who had to go into the lion's den first. And anything could have happened. These boys played rough; they didn't have to beat them that bad. Now I could have five serious enemies to think about.

I realised then that my dependence on the organisation was growing day by day, not so much by my own making but by the way it operated, putting you in such a position that you needed its support, and I didn't like it.

Wherever you go, there's some cunt or other trying to make you dependent on them.

I thought about it long and hard on the way back to the West End, watching all the other dependants carrying their briefcases and toolbags to and from work. Who were worse, my cunts or their cunts? These animals sitting around me with their baseball bats or those animals out there hiding behind well-polished office doors destroying people legally? Why couldn't I fit in anywhere?

This thing that lurked inside me, this thing that caused me to be so unreasonably anti-social, was going to set me apart from everyone. When it came down to it, I didn't want to be a part of anything, legal or illegal, right or wrong, good or bad. I wanted to be a free agent among free agents. There had to be somewhere I could go.

I gave myself another year.

As time passed by and I became more and more part of the organisation, I realised that the core of Vince's security business was based on what others called a 'protection racket'. Clients paid for this security and in return were protected from other racketeers or troublemakers, but most of these clients had little say in the matter and had usually been enrolled by thinly disguised threat. Anyone refusing the services offered soon found that they needed protection, and it was me that collected the payments.

Around this central business a whole network of other businesses existed, spreading all over London and beyond, as far north as Glasgow and across the Channel to Europe. As far as I could make out, Vince was just the top man of this one section and everywhere you looked there were other Vinces, most of them carrying on their business from behind a respectable cover.

Earlier, before I'd been recruited, I'd believed that crime was an isolated thing the forces of law and order kept at bay, but now I saw that crime was just another way of life that existed hand in hand with so-called 'normal' life, and that the people who got nicked, apart from kids, idiots and social misfits, were usually carrying the can for the leaders of these criminal organisations. These high-ups held far too much information on important public figures to be dragged into the dock for interrogation, so someone else always stood in when the public started screaming for blood.

Say what you like about Vince, but it didn't pay to work freelance. One day I read in the paper that Sheila from Hackney, the girl we used to roll punters with, had been found carved up. She was referred to as a 'prostitute' and I suddenly recalled her innocence the first time we'd used the Regent Palace Hotel. Now she was dead, a victim of circumstance: if I hadn't met her at La Discothèque, she might still be alive now, working in a shop or something, instead of being in pieces in a morgue, the third victim of the latest pervert on the scene.

Despite these occasional horrors, I loved my life, if only for the girls I met and the amount of respect I got from the clubbers who knew that I had a flat in Soho. But I made sure to steer clear of Vince's inner circle because I didn't want to get any more involved than was necessary, especially now that I'd given myself a year.

During time off I got out of London and drove down to Margate and Brighton again to see old friends, or took Monica away somewhere so that Vince and his mates couldn't get hold of me for any more of their dirty work – not that I minded brawling, if it was spontaneous, but cold-blooded violence wasn't really my number. A couple of weeks after the Lewisham thing I'd been part of another team that suddenly had to visit a gambling club to 'put in a presence', as they would have it, but again it ended in tears with someone getting shot. Despite my protests that I wasn't really needed on these visits, Vince thought it was good education for me. 'Stick by me, son,' he'd say, 'and I'll see you're all right.' How many times have I heard that sentiment dressed up in different disguises?

As summer established itself, I took more and more time off in Margate, driving down with Frankie and Jacko or Micky or someone else, and the relief to be away and just playing again with friends, away from the dealings of deranged men, was exhilarating. Again I could behave like I wanted to behave, like a nineteen-year-old. I could fight and shag and show off and take drugs and drink too much, but most of all I could be my own boss.

NINE

MARGATE

Margate was a small seaside town with a short main seafront dominated by cafés and amusement arcades. At one end the road veered inland past Westcliff into a boring maze of houses and council estates, and at the other it divided at the clocktower, the upper road leading into the town centre and the lower more or less following the shoreline up to Cliftonville, a cliff-top resort almost as depressing as Westcliff.

By the clocktower was a basement club, the Tahiti, and at the other end of the promenade, the Westcliff end, sat the Dreamland Dance Hall, an ugly building designed to spoil the look of the seafront. Between these two points and the many old and interesting pubs all over town we constantly circulated in the never-ending search for entertainment and stimulation.

Rockers were by now an almost extinct breed, having been driven out of most towns across the country by fast-growing gangs of Mods who, encouraged by the anti-hero image they'd been handed on a plate by the media, were running riot just about everywhere. From time to time the odd band of Rockers showed up and hung around just long enough to attract attention, but in the main their days were numbered. The other reason for their demise, of course, was that most girls who had anything going for them wouldn't be seen dead with a Rocker, and the only way round this for them, if they wanted anything to do with the breeding process, was to change sides and join the mob.

As more and more of these ex-Rockers became 'Mods', so the distinct type became blurred and more outsiders were able to find their way into what had once been an exclusive club. 'Mods' with DA haircuts and pointed shoes walked about unmolested, and altogether unsuitable characters began to hang out in what were once Mod strongholds.

One weekend we stopped to pick up Micky from a pub just outside London before we went on down to Margate. With him was a bloke who had just come out of prison and needed a bit of rehabilitation, a sort of ex-spiv who Micky said would be a laugh to go drinking with, but Frankie wasn't so sure. 'I don't know about you,' he said to me on the side, 'but I'm not walking about with anyone wearing a whistle like that.'

He had a point. His grey worsted suit was like something from the late fifties: narrow trousers with two-inch slits either side, and a double-breasted bumfreezer jacket like my uncles used to wear. The poor man had been left in a time warp by his spell inside.

As luck would have it, more friends showed and he went in their car, but it would have been far better for everybody if Micky hadn't convinced him that a weekend in Margate was what he needed to get back into the swing of things.

As we drove out on to the Kentish roads that fine summer evening, none of us realised just where we were heading.

* * *

Two cars, nine geezers in tailored suits, expensive after-shave, pockets full of money, change of clothes in the boot, lairy.

Westcliff-on-Sea dark and miserable as usual, past the semi-detached houses and featureless estates and out into the million coloured lights and teeming human shoals of Margate seafront. We shout through the car's open windows at smiling crumpet, arranging to meet later, and a male figure comes flying backwards through the double doors of the Cinque Ports pub.

'Here we go,' says Frankie quietly, staring deadpan at the bleeding figure sprawled on the Yorkstone paving.

A lone motorbike passes at speed, followed by a bottle, which smashes alongside the car.

'Oi, watch where you're fucking slinging them bottles, you dozy cunt!' I shout to one of a group of new Mods.

'Sorry, mate,' he says, alarmed, and his mates turn away from him, body language for 'you're on your own now'.

Frankie wants to jump out and lump him but I drive on towards the busy clocktower, where we can park behind the public gardens and get in the pub on the corner. We can save the Cinque Ports for later. But first it's a quick look inside the Tahiti to see who's about.

The other car with Micky and co. has already disappeared. It's the way we usually do it: split up and move in from different sides, ambush the town.

We go down the blue palm-tree stairs and into the dark jangling 'Baby Love' pounding Motown room. Baby Love Ooh I Need Your Love. The Tahiti is full of shitters – baby girls with tits who shit out when it comes to shagging – and cocky Greek kids whose family owns the premises and baby Mods and older ones being worshipped by some of the locals who haven't quite sussed the styles yet.

My superb oyster Tonik suit responds vibrantly to the lighting and I enter the room like Flash Gordon and light a cigarette. Frankie says, 'Gis one, yer cunt,' so I have to hand them round to Peter and Baz as well, who are with us, and a shitter who appears to have latched on who calls herself Caroline and keeps smiling.

Martin from Margate is there, sitting in a corner surrounded by local friends, and we score some French blues for the crack, but I now prefer shagging, having been trained and guided carefully past the pitfalls of adolescent sex by Monica. There is nothing better than shagging, being as rude as possible with members of the opposite sex, and I scan the females present, looking for promising eye contact. Those who do not respond are from then on ruthlessly ignored to avoid time-wasting and possible loss of face if they tell you to fuck off. The best come-on, however, is still from shitter, who looks about fifteen or sixteen but is, on further consideration, developing very nicely.

We have to leave to get a room in a guest house before they all put up 'No Vacancies' signs, so the four of us emerge from the basement, walk a hundred yards and get two rooms in a sleazy guest house called the Thanet Hotel, me and Frankie in one and Pete and Baz in the other.

We stand looking at sunken single beds. Clean but well-worn. But these people take the piss, do they not? After snobbing it with Monica around the West End, I know what a decent room looks like. Frankie takes the bed nearest the window from which you can see and hear Dreamland Fairground across the rooftops: multi-coloured flashing lights, spinning and screaming, and loud-speaking calls to try your skill or spend your money on the thrill of a lifetime.

I go to car to fetch fighting clothes in case they are needed, but decide to stay suited to impress for the time being.

'Baby love, my baby love
Baby love ooh I need your love . . .'

We leave, locking door behind us, and walk up through crowds to corner pub. Meet Pete and Baz and Jacko, who has left Micky and co. – including geezer who is just out of prison: 'Birdman', as we now call him – to do their own thing, and begin drinking. Five light and bitters thank you very much.

But pub is not friendly and after ten minutes local hairy bastards knock into Baz, who reacts, and a fight starts. Tables go over, bottles fly and we are up against the whole pub, who are all locals resenting flash strangers. A small, fat woman, the landlord's wife, tries to smash a large china ashtray on my head, but I duck and she misses; then she attacks me and tries to claw my face, shrieking at me, accusing me of punching her husband, which is true, so I seize her hands and spin round and round until her little piggy feet leave the ground and cut a swathe through the brawling crowd. I let go because she's screaming hysterically, and she flies through the door and lands in a heap on the pavement outside, where a crowd has gathered to watch. Soon the locals, discovering just how fucking nasty we can be, have fled or are lying about on the floor groaning and bleeding, and the publican is apologising, yes, apologising, to us for the absent bastards who he says started it. But really he is frightened and Baz is screaming something about burning the place down to teach the cunts a lesson. The publican's wife is sobbing uncontrollably in the corner, being soothed by a platinum-blonde slag who, like the whore of a defeated man, is showing out strongly, especially to Jacko. Earlier she'd squeezed his bum, and he is considering a victory knee-trembler outside while her male is hiding somewhere. 'Look after my beer,' he's saying, 'while I go and give it one.'

Unscathed and extra flash, we accept free placatory drinks, which we down quickly, surrounded by wreckage and still observed by crowd outside, then fuck off quick before Old Bill arrives to stir up locals again. Jacko disappears with platinum-blonde woman.

Cinque Ports is a nice old pub but dangerous, being on the corner outside Dreamland, and fights always happen. Shortly after we arrive, one starts in the lower bar. It lasts for about ten minutes until the floor is strewn with bodies, but we find a group of female friends and stay with them in the upper bar, occasionally going to have a look through the door to see how things are going. During all this, Jacko comes back looking pleased with himself and describes the shag using terms such as 'she couldn't get enough of it' and 'couldn't keep her off of me' and 'give it a right fucking seeing to', and I picture her male hiding somewhere while this is happening and get strange mixed feelings about it.

Other people we know from London come and go all night as they move from pub to pub, and outside only the younger Mods who can't get in the pubs are still trying to drum up some sort of anti-Rocker passion.

At closing time we turn out and pair off with the girls and disappear into the night, me and my sort towards the nice part of Margate where she lives with her mummy and daddy, which is all Regency squares and people who think they are a cut above the rest. But my girl doesn't and I really think she is special, a real good-looker and truly nice – but she won't let me past her parents' front door. To appease me she says that I can come in tomorrow instead because they are going to be away, and I vow to myself never to live by the seaside and have daughters.

So now what? I've blown a night taking it for granted that I was on to a good thing. I walk back along the still-teeming neon front to the Tahiti, and back down the pounding stairs. It's Sam the Sham and Woolly Bully now – shame they've never heard of Blue Beat in these parts.

Give me Jamaica ska any day. Micky and Birdman are there with others, but Birdman is concentrating on shitters like his sort just out of nick would – cell-wall fantasies coming to life; flesh-and-blood virgins waiting breathlessly and doe-eyed, he thinks, for a hand-calloused dick.

Word goes round there's a party in a doss-house over at the back of town so we go and the place is a complete shit-hole. On the wall is painted CLIVE'S MAD-HOUSE because someone called Clive who lives near me in London seems to be running the place. All night, people just move from room to room, blocked, and Birdman takes too many dubes and begins to get on people's nerves, talking strangely, out of touch with everybody. Then he asks a little sort to go for a walk with him and everyone is relieved when they go, not realising that he is going to murder her.

No one is aware that he is about to become unbalanced by the chemicals he has ingested, the alcohol and amphe-tamines he has swallowed in a desperate attempt to blur the prison mentality and the inadequacy he feels every time he opens his mouth.

Even we find it difficult to keep up with ourselves.

He, a generation older, is a man lost on the brink of amphetamine madness.

Still pill-free, I walk back to the guest house and go to bed. I do not want to risk impotence with my Regency-square bird. Frankie is out somewhere, his bed untouched.

Next morning I put on white Levis with starting pistol in belt, grey woollen polo shirt and black boxing boots and go out along sunny seafront to observe the overnight beach kippers looking bedraggled and smelly. I go in Italian café which does good breakfasts and find all the others there.

You heard about Birdman? What about him? Done a little sortie in when he left the 'madhouse' – you remember that little sortie? What do you mean 'done a little sortie in'? Murdered her. Fucking stroll on – how do you know? I mean, who told you this? The Old Bill are all over the place. They came and interviewed us all. He strangled her – they found her clothes all over the park. He couldn't have fucked her, though, too blocked. Cunt. Yeah, reckon he did about twenty. Is that all? Cunt. Fucking said you shouldn't have brought him. Fucking geezer's a nut-case. Have they got him yet? Give himself up. Probably on a comedown wondering what's happened. I don't fucking believe it. Reporters give me and Jacko a tenner each for our stories – a fucking tenner! What did you tell them? Any old shit. Told them loads of bollocks about sex and drugs and they swallowed it all.

Now it's a long wait for the boozers to open.

Think about it.

Little girl's dead.

Little Hastings boy's dead.

Dinger's dead.

We walk along in the seafront sunshine, six of us and some girls. We join up with a big crew by the clocktower and talk about murder. It does nothing to me. It's getting regular now. I wonder how they're going to call this one an accident. A cry of 'Rockers' goes up as a growling cluster of bikes drives by and some give chase, but it's a small thing and the bikes drive on out. We hear that one of the lairy Greeks has been done over and someone's fallen off a cliff in the night, but still more important is opening time.

There's an hour to go, so we walk back along the front as the day-trippers and late arrivals pour in. There's a strong atmosphere of lawlessness, and stale vomit and spilt beer and chips and hot dogs and frying onions and deodorant and disinfectant, and we drift into Dreamland Fairground and walk about on the already hot tarmac between the stalls and rides and stand and watch skirted women in the House of Horror walk over the updraught to display their white legs and drawers to the world. To one side a scuffle between kids has caused a small diversion, and to the other a gang of girls is taking the dodgems by storm. Micky runs and jumps on the back of one of the cars, but seeing that he is part of an insane gang the dodgems minder says nothing. When they stop we join together and head for the Cinque Ports, arriving as the doors are unlocked.

In we pour, ordering pints and vodkas and brandies, and our lairiness is unsurpassed as these drinks vanish and are quickly replaced, until a sense of well-being fills us and the bar. This promises to be a wonderful, sunny, momentous day for those who aren't bereaved. Then another gang arrives and I recognise one of them as an old schoolmate, and as our groups amalgamate we dominate the whole pub and are invincible. One of schoolmate's gang is a lunatic who gets his willy out and chases the girls around the bar with it, stretching the foreskin out in front like a half-inflated Christmas balloon, and the grand finale is when he lies on the floor in front of the entrance and wanks for fun, pulling mad faces at the ceiling, at which point the door opens and there stands an old couple, popping in for a brown and mild and a Mackeson.

'Ooh I say!' she says.

'Well!' he says. 'Come on, dear, we'll go somewhere else.'

They turn about and close the door gently behind them as screams of laughter fill the air.

Regency-square bird comes in looking stunning and I am very pleased when her face lights up as she sees me. Her friend is also very tasty and they are momentarily the centre of attention as lunatic prances around them with his dick, but they just take a look at it and laugh sweetly like angels.

When we turn out late at three o'clock, the sun is shining fiercely and the whole of Margate is like a distant glaring film set, so we escape into Dreamland Dance Hall for the afternoon, where big bouncers strut about looking serious, trying to intimidate.

Sedated by light and bitter, I dance closely with Regency and can feel an erection coming on. My only desire is to share it with her as soon as possible and I whisper through her scented hair loving things, enquiring whether her parents have gone away yet. She says they have and that it would be cool to go back and we head towards the door and slide away for hours of steamy sex.

Her house is large, with a grandish entrance, and once over the threshold we begin fierce snogging. We stagger to the stairs and continue there, groping, but she is suddenly horrified as my fingers search too far and stops, appearing to sober up, and starts crying. The hot sun is beaming down on us through a skylight over the stairwell. Confused, I look at her gorgeous face all splodged with black, her beautiful eyes full of liquid, and wonder what I've done. She says she's never done anything like this before and she is ashamed and embarrassed so I say sorry, maybe next time, and leave.

Back in the dance hall the mood has changed to one of simmering hate as the bouncers push their luck, and it isn't long before breaking glass heralds the start of another battle. Overwhelmed by the numbers, they regroup in the entrance and call the police, trapping us all inside, but I have the answer to this in the waistband of my Levis.

Approaching the line of bouncers blocking the exit, I give them an ultimatum to move and let everyone out or else, but they stand shoulder to shoulder looking resolute, so I pull the gun from my waistband. 'Okay, get out of the fucking way!' I scream. As if by magic they part, leaving a gap for everyone to file through until just four of us stand there facing a dozen unsure bouncers. Jacko shouts, 'Shoot the cunts!' and I pull the trigger again and again, shooting at anyone who hasn't thrown himself on the deck. Then we run out on to the crowded promenade and I let loose another couple of shots for effect and sprint away through the gaping day-trippers and into the back alleys of town.

There are Old Bill everywhere now, and I'm still running when no one's watching, walking casually when someone's around. But worried should I get a pull, I shove the gun underneath a garage door and stroll casually away in the direction of Cliftonville.

I find a clean piece of lawn in the flower gardens and, suddenly overcome by alcohol fatigue, lie down and fall asleep in the shade of an overhanging bush. To go back to the guest house at this stage would be stupid, wouldn't it?

The ground beneath me becomes damp and unfriendly, saying, 'Get up and fuck off somewhere else,' and the warming sun has disappeared behind the grim tenements they call guest houses in this part of the world, casting a darkening shadow into the sea beyond the cliffs. Below, Margate is beginning to twinkle again as evening creeps in, so I stand up and brush the lawn trimmings from my elbows and clothing before setting out back downhill for the pubs.

Halfway down I meet Margate Martin and some friends and we swallow a few pints of beer in the nearest pub. I down half a dozen French blues to liven me up and before I realise what has happened the publican's calling time and I've done nothing.

I trot back into town to see if I can find anyone, but as I arrive at the guest-house street I see a police car outside and retreat back up past clocktower – more police – and continue on towards Cliftonville and the all-night bowling alley, always a good place to hang out if you're a boring fucker with nowhere better to go. At least I can get a cup of tea there.

But the night is now beginning to take on a strangely hostile tone and inside Excel Bowling I cannot find a single familiar face. I've stepped outside of my own world. This face in front of me is ugly but I ask it the time and its owner stares at his thick bare wrist and says 'don't know' and laughs. 'Fucking funnyman,' I say, and he asks if I want to make anything of it. I stare at him, for the first time realising that he means business, he and his two pals, and wants to hurt me in some way. Others stop to watch and I realise that I have strayed into no man's land where the hyenas, jackals and rats live. Now it's comeuppance time unless I can get out quick.

Bravado. Show no fear. Confront the pack. Confront the leader. I look at him again: mid to late twenties, a bit taller than me, fit and muscular, and very, very ugly. Ex-Rocker, by the look of his trimmed Elvis hairstyle. 'Yeah,' I says, 'I'll make something of it. When do you want it, now or later?' This allows him to back out without losing face by saying something like 'I'll have you later, you cunt' before walking away. But instead his eyes light up and he says, 'Now'll do me. I'll see you round the back.' And off he goes.

By this time a largish neutral crowd has formed to watch and any chance of sliding away has disappeared. 'You want to be careful, mate, he's hard,' says one. 'No he's not,' says another. 'He's in the army,' says a third. 'You can do him,' says my worst enemy in the world at that moment, a stranger who is probably worried that I'll back out and deny him the pleasure of watching a bit of bloodshed.

But a cocktail of half a dozen French blues, six pints of

ale and a fit body does not allow for retreat, and I stride after my antagonist into the cool night air.

Behind the building I see a crowd beneath a street lamp. He is waiting at the edge, suddenly looking even more menacing than he did inside, flexing his hands and fingers and shifting his weight from foot to foot like a professional fighter. The element of surprise is always useful, so without preamble or pause to discuss the rules I walk straight up to him and catch him by surprise with a fair punch in the eye. He staggers back, which gives me the chance to follow up the attack, kicking and punching, but then I lose it, thinking that he isn't all that strong, and stupidly try to throw him to the ground to finish him off. But if only . . .

If only I hadn't forgotten my boxing training and reverted to playground wrestling where size and muscle mean everything, I might just have been able to hold him off.

But now I am in his hands and, well, I've had it.

Slowly he gathers his strength and lifts me from the ground, then throws me on to my back, knocking the wind from my lungs. Leaping on to me with a mean grin on his face, he begins trying to smash my skull on the cobblestones, and but for one of the onlookers who thinks that enough's enough and pulls him off, he would probably have been up for murder.

Back on my feet, I stagger about dazed and try blurting out threats like losers do but am thankful for the support and sympathy I can just make out seeping slowly into my jarred brain cells. As the satisfied crowd slowly drifts away chatting, I can smell cheap perfume and hear soft words of care and tenderness: 'It's all right,' they say. 'Don't worry. My mum and dad have got a beach hut, you can rest in there.'

And when I begin to see straight again and look at where the sweet female words are coming from, I see the little shitter from the Tahiti, Caroline, standing there, staring into my eyes with adoration.

'You feeling any better?' she asks as she guides me slowly across the road towards the beach.

'Yeah, yeah, cheers.' I manage to laugh. 'Good job someone stopped him.'

'I asked one of my friends to stop it. I've seen him before. He just goes around picking on people.'

'Cunt. Who is he then?'

'He's in the marines.'

'Fuck's sake.' My head begins throbbing.

'I think his wife's just left him as well . . .'

'Don't blame her.'

Of all the people I meet when I'm not team-handed, it has to be a fucking marine commando with marriage problems. Bigger, stronger and meaner than me. Learn, boy, learn.

I hold my head.

'You all right?' she asks again in that young-girl softness, and I wonder if perhaps I can overcome the effects of just six French blues. She might be young but she's pretty.

'What's it like in your mum and dad's beach hut?'

'It's quite nice,' she says, keen. 'There's a little cooker and a water container and tea and stuff, and two little bunks either side if you want to lie down.'

'Room for two?'

She looks pleased. 'If you put the two mattresses on the floor.'

'Come on then. Come and show me.' My headache disappears miraculously, and we set out with renewed energy for the beach.

Finding a box of matches, she lights a gas lamp and I'm able to see the inside of a beach hut for the first time. Her parents obviously think a lot of it, keeping it as clean and well decorated as most people keep their homes. She pulls the door to and bolts it.

'Sit down,' she says. 'Shall I make some tea?'

'No. Come and sit next to me and give me a cuddle. I need looking after.'

And the night dissolves into a dim-lit memory of over-passionate kissing and breathless groping as we try to overcome the merciless amphetamine demon.

'It's no good. We'll have to wait a bit.'

'I don't mind. Do you want a cigarette?'

'Cheers.'

I examine her pretty face again by matchlight – she could grow up to be a stunner or a fat cunt; there's no telling when they're young – and look at her small breasts inside a white young-teens bra. She isn't shy for a youngster. We are still both more or less fully clothed, but undone.

'D'you take pills a lot?' she asks.

'Used to. But this is the first time for ages.'

'Can't see the point if this is what it does to you.'

'You never taken them?'

'No. I like life enough as it is.'

'But if you go up the West End and stay up from Friday night until Monday night, you need them to stay awake.'

'I'd rather go to bed.'

We smoke in silence for a bit, then I ask her how old she is.

'Fifteen.'

'And still at school?'

'Yeah.'

'You a virgin?'

'You'll have to find out.'

'You're not, are you?' I laugh.

'That's my business . . . anyway, what difference does it make?'

'Fucking hell . . .' I can't think of anything else to say.

'What's wrong with being a virgin?'

'I'm not saying there's anything wrong with it. Where do your mum and dad think you are tonight?'

'Around my friend's . . .' She looks as if she is about to say something.

'What's up?' I ask. Walking the streets was beginning to get dangerous for young girls. Maybe she knew the one Birdman had met. But it wouldn't be cool to tell her he had come down with us.

'Don't you want to . . . I mean . . . am I too young?' she asks, looking down her nose.

So that was it. 'No, it's the pills, I told you.'

We smoke on, and suddenly I feel desperately sad for all the females of the world.

'Did you hear about that girl who got murdered?' she asks.

'I think everyone has. Did you know her?'

'Yeah. Not very well. She wasn't much older than me.'

'Fuck's sake.' It doesn't really strike home until you're faced with someone you can compare it with. 'What was she like?'

'All right. But she hung around with older blokes a lot.'

'Like you do, you mean?'

'No – he was twenty-eight. How old are you?'

'Twenty-one.' I always lied about my age.

This was one of the things they were saying, that she hung around with older blokes, but I didn't see what difference that made. Society was always trying to make excuses for its fuck-ups. Oh yeah, they were saying, what do you expect, carrying on like that? Going about with older blokes. Shameful. Disgusting. Then there was the other view about him, going about with young girls. A man his age ought to know better, fucking pervert.

181

But he was shaped by his background, like all of us, and so was she, and between themselves and the moonlight they created their own little nightmare.

'I don't see what difference that makes,' I add.

'What?'

'Him being twenty-eight.'

'No, I suppose not.'

'Do you prefer older blokes?'

'Most girls do,' she says, drawing closer as the night gets cooler.

We put out our cigarettes and start again.

At some time just before dawn we get there, but it is a messy business and deals my taste for amphetamines another damaging blow.

Also, Caroline has begun menstruating and has covered the front of my white Levis with blood, so I have to wash them in the cold early-morning sea, wring them out and wear them until I get back to the Thanet Hotel, where I can change.

* * *

In the guest house I fell on the bed and slept fitfully, waking again in the late morning of what was to be another sunny day. I sat on the edge of the bed and yawned, running my fingers through my hair, trying to pick up on the night – the bowling alley brought back memories I couldn't bear to face, memories of defeat and a shattered ego; thinking of Caroline made me feel inadequate and low. Friday's dreams had disintegrated, and I was left with Monday's emptiness and bruises.

After washing and changing I set out for Mario's Café for a late breakfast, and there I met Frankie and Liz, a little blonde from Bexley who attracted me in a big way. I should have realised I was partially concussed and wholly unstable, but when you are you don't, so we sat and ate and flirted and touched danger zone with Frankie, who, although seemingly unaware of what was going on, was a dodgy person to mess about with. But females were my life; I couldn't stop now. Every chance I had I took, sending signals across the table that couldn't be misunderstood.

It might have ended there had Frankie and Liz moved on, but as if to court danger he suddenly spotted someone outside the café he needed to speak to and rushed off, shouting that he'd meet us later in the Cinque Ports. So we were alone, and I came straight to the point.

'Do you realise I've fallen madly in love and badly need to fuck you?' I said.

Did I really say that? My mouth seemed to have developed a mind of its own since my head's collision with the cobblestones.

'Oh, I know,' she said, before I could get embarrassed. 'It happens to me all the time.'

'I don't doubt it. How could anyone resist you?'

'They can't.'

'Flash cow. Come on, let's run away together. Come and see my room.'

She laughed. '*Me* flash! And there's you coming on strong to your best mate's bird.'

'You're not Frankie's bird.'

'How do you know what I am?'

'I know you're not his bird because you've only just met him, silly. Anyway, we were meant for each other.'

'Is that right?' she said, looking all enticing.

'Come on! Where do you fancy going?'

'You're a cheeky sod, aren't you?' she said.

'Not at all. *Come on*, where shall we go?' She was up for it, there was no doubt about that.

'Oh, I don't mind,' she said. 'Let's go for a drink some-where.'

I'd pulled. Whoopee. A nice sortie as well. The sort of bird you could take anywhere instead of having to keep hidden away. Jacko's got a secret dolly he goes to see every now and again just for the legover, when he's got nothing better to do. I don't know why she puts up with it. Although I suppose you could look at it the other way and say that she's using him. Then there's Frankie and Norma; she's not really on the game any more, but he just sees her when he's stuck for something to do. And then there's Baz, who goes round to shag Gerry Plumley's bird when he's out.

I paid for the three breakfasts, wondering whether I'd been had over, and we went for a walk along the seafront towards Dreamland. Just as we reached the entrance I uncharacteristically forgot about Frankie and turned and kissed her on the mouth. She responded enthusiastically with closed eyes and a thrust of the crutch, and I was just thinking how sweet her mouth tasted even after a full breakfast, two cups of tea and three Embassy Filters when our teeth clashed violently as someone punched me hard in the back of the head.

Spinning around, I saw an enraged Frankie swinging another punch, but before he could land it I side-stepped and countered with a combination to the head which knocked him flat on his back. I wasn't going to suffer another beat-ing in one weekend. As he tried to get up I kicked him hard in the ribs and head, sending him sprawling again, and rushed in to finish him off, but invisible hands from a gathering crowd of passers-by grabbed me from behind and hung on, giving him time to jump up and attack again while my arms were being held.

Maddened by now, I broke loose and again punched

Frankie away, then turned on the crowd and began lashing out at anyone within reach. Like sheep they panicked and tried to escape into what was by now becoming a large audience, causing old ladies and children to get trampled underfoot. Turning back quickly to concentrate on Frankie, I saw that he had run into an open-fronted restaurant packed with diners and was looking for a weapon, but the waiters had barred his way to the knife box and he turned to see me in pursuit. Shoving aside a stunned family halfway through their plaice and chips, he jumped up on the table and launched himself at me like someone in a brawl at the Last Chance Saloon, but his timing was bad and I caught him mid-air with a right-hander which knocked him back through the front of the restaurant and out into the street again. Dashing after him, upturning loaded tables on the way, I caught him with a hard kick to the jaw as he knelt on all fours trying to regain his senses, and it all but finished him, but again I was seized from behind, this time by Jacko and Baz, who'd come out of the Cinque Ports pub to see what all the noise was about.

'Tommy! Tommy!' Jacko was shouting. 'Stop, you cunt! What's the matter with the pair of you? You'll have the Old Bill here in a minute.'

But now Frankie was coming back again, to screams from the crowd, wielding a vinegar bottle he'd snatched from a table. They had to let me free to defend myself, but Baz knocked the bottle away, sending it crashing to the ground, and head-butted Frankie, giving me a chance to throw Jacko out of the way and counterattack.

Then suddenly it was over. Frankie had seen the tall, dark-blue helmets of the police and shouted 'Old Bill' to me before disappearing into the crowd. Following his lead, I walked innocently past them and into the pub. Little Liz from Bexley, well, she probably had enough sense to realise that there wasn't going to be a lot of mileage in either of us. We never saw her again.

The sum total of the wild weekend at Margate came to: the destruction of two sets of clothes, a black eye and a fat lip, and a dose of NSU from dear little Caroline for which I had to suffer treatment at Guy's Hospital under the smirking gaze of a doctor and six students, both male and female. As I lay flat on my back with my pants around my ankles, the doctor inserted a loop of fine wire into the end of my penis, twisted it and smeared the collected matter on to a glass slide which he placed under a microscope for each of them to study in turn. I tried giving the come-on to one of the girls with a covert wink, but she didn't seem to want to know.

TEN

DOG FOOD

Back in London, I learnt that I'd lost Monica to a Lebanese millionaire. She came to see me and said that she was getting engaged and that it was time to call it a day. You wouldn't believe it, but I was choked. From then on my interest in work decreased almost daily until Vince came to see me with a mad glint in his eye, and I could see something was up.

Sitting down on the single chair in my room, he began by asking why takings had fallen, and I didn't beat about the bush.

'Because I'm getting fed up with being a rent collector, Vince. I thought that I was coming in with you to get involved in some serious business, like buying and selling cars or houses or something – you know, something I could maybe get into and then, with a bit of help from you, start up on my own, that sort of thing. Rent collecting's not my scene.'

He stared at me. 'Who gave you the shiner?'

'I got it in a ruck down at Margate.'

'Margate. Fucking Margate. What's the matter with you boys? Here I am doing my best for you, trying to bring you into a team that's involved with all sorts of interesting sidelines, and all you want to do is waste your time sniffing around the arsehole of England. I hope you gave as good as you got.'

'Better.'

'Good.' He paused. 'You say you want to get involved in more interesting work.'

'Yeah. Something where I don't feel like a thieving bastard every time I walk out of the punter's door.'

'Okay. As it happens, the main reason I've come to see you is that I've got a little one-off that'll be right up your street. How do you fancy that?'

'What is it? I don't fancy any more of those visiting parties. I'm getting a bad name.'

'Look, Tommy, the nature of this business means that we have to lean on people from time to time. Don't go soft on me.'

'Leave it out. You make me feel like a prick. I'm not going soft on you, Vince, I just need a change. Don't get me wrong, I appreciate everything you've done for me.'

'Now you're talking. I just told you I had a nice little job lined up for you, didn't I? Trust me – I think you'll like it. Have you got a pen?'

I found a pen and gave it to him.

Tearing a small strip of paper from the edge of an *Evening Standard,* he laboriously wrote something on it. My boss and he can't even write. There's something sad about big men who can't write properly.

'Here,' he said. 'Bring yourself along to this address tomorrow evening at seven. Wear old gear and bring a change of clothes with you, all right?'

That's all I needed now, a demotion to painter and decorator. If that's what it turns out to be, I thought, I'm jacking it in, there and then. And if he don't like it, tough. I'd rather go and sell papers on the street corner.

'Vince,' I said, looking at him askance, 'if you're taking the piss . . .'

He laughed aloud, squeezed my knee, then stood up. 'Trust me, I said. Trust me.' Then he turned and walked out.

The following evening I made my way to what looked like a small factory hidden neatly down a track several hundred yards off one of the main roads leading out of London.

I parked outside next to a couple of other cars, picked up my bag containing the change of clothes and went and rang the bell. A stranger answered and I told him who I was. Without a word he led me through a reception area with a desk and switchboard into the rear of the building, which, going by the white tiles and smell, appeared to be some sort of food factory. Stopping at a cloakroom, he told me to change into my old clothing, then gave me an overall to wear. 'Leave your clothes hanging in here,' he said.

Then we went through into a larger room. To one side was an office with half-glazed walls, and through them I could make out Vince and a couple of other blokes.

I was shown in.

'Tommy, my son!' exclaimed Vince when he saw me. 'How are you? Take a seat. This is Teddy and this is Aitch.' He eyed my overall up and down. 'You'll never make a foreman looking like that.'

I shook their hands, first Teddy, with his peroxided curly hair and a false-tanned lizard face, who was without doubt a queen, and then Aitch, who looked like an off-duty insurance salesman. The man who'd shown me in went back out the way we had come.

Vince went on. 'Right. Now we're all present, I'll quickly fill in your backgrounds to each other, then we'll go through into the factory where it'll become clear, especially to you, Tommy, what this is all about. Teddy and Aitch know the score already about what's going on, but I'll go through it again for your benefit. First of all, Teddy here is what we call in the business a "male performer", you know what I mean?' He looked at me questioningly.

'Yeah – like the geezers you see in the Garden of Eden.'

'That's it, but our Teddy's famous on the circuit for his large hampton. Don't look so worried – it'll all become clear to you.' He laughed. 'Do you want to see it? Have a look, it'll make your eyes water.'

Teddy gasped in false modesty. 'Vince!' he squealed. 'Not in front of the nice young man.'

This was getting very strange. 'Thanks all the same,' I said, glancing at the doors and windows and wondering whether to try and make a run for it. Was the glass plate or just the ordinary stuff? Would I bounce back off if I tried to leap through it, or cut myself to ribbons and die in a pool of blood?

They all laughed at my obvious discomfort.

Vince carried on. 'Anyway, plenty of time for that. And Aitch is a movie photographer specialising in educational films. We've already set up his equipment next door.' He looked at Teddy and Aitch. 'Tommy, as I've already said, is here for a bit of light entertainment, but we need him to put us right on your . . . er . . . co-star, Teddy, okay?'

So that was it. Porno films. As long as I wasn't expected to be part of it. And why did they need me to advise them on his co-star? Was it a she or a he?

'Okay, lads,' said Vince. 'Let's go.' Teddy picked up an overnight bag he had by his side as Vince ushered us out of the office like a rich uncle and led us across the room to a door.

'Where are the girls?' I asked him.

'No girls, son,' said Vince, suddenly serious. 'Just Teddy and his co-star.'

Definitely a queer job. The hairs were beginning to stand up on the back of my neck. What if they were going to shag me? What could I have done to piss Vince off? Surely not. Maybe he was queer too. Perhaps I was walking into an all-male orgy.

Teddy winked and smiled.

I couldn't. I couldn't.

'I'm not too sure I'm up to this, Vince,' I said, hoping he'd relent and send me home. I thought of my mum and dad – I should have known when I was well off. Fuck this.

I looked about again, but there was definitely no way out. The windows here were barred, and the only other door was guarded by a minder.

Vince opened the door and we walked into a large room like a coldstore with hooks and racking on the ceiling. The walls were white-tiled and the floors concrete, a strange enough setting for a porno film, but in the centre stood a butcher's wooden block, alone and sinister, with a little stack of leather belts and a bucketful of water to one side. Facing this, at a distance of about four yards, were four director's chairs, a powerful studio light and a movie camera on a tripod.

'Take a seat, boys,' said Vince, and we all sat down. I began to tremble. Something was very odd about all this. What the fuck was I doing here? Why me?

Vince clapped his hands sharply and from a blind corner to our right came the sound of scuffling and the voice of someone very angry. It sounded vaguely familiar. 'I'm telling you! If you don't fucking let me go, you're going to be sorry for this. I fucking mean it! Let me go, you arseholes!'

It couldn't be. No way. But . . .

Two men in white overalls, masks and hats appeared, dragging a dark figure between them. A figure in a studded leather jacket. A figure that at one time had given me sleepless nights.

Kenser!

They dragged him across the room and stopped at the block, holding him there facing us, and for a while nothing was said as he tried to squint past the lights at us. Aitch stood up and set the camera in motion. Then Vince spoke.

'Are you Kenser Donnelly?'

Kenser hesitated. 'No,' he lied.

'Yes you fucking are!' I said loudly, surprising myself.

'Good boy,' said Vince to me. Looking back at Kenser, he pronounced, 'The prisoner's identity is established. Kenser Donnelly . . .'

'Yeah, yeah, okay, I'm fucking Kenser Donnelly. What the fuck's all this about?'

'One more interruption,' said Vince, 'and we'll break one of your arms. Do you understand?'

This was getting scarier by the second. Vince would do it. And if he would break one of his arms at this stage, just to shut him up, what did he have planned for later? The thought of having to watch another systematic hospital-isation turned my stomach.

But Kenser wouldn't shut up. 'Fuck you!' he screamed. 'I haven't done anything! Let me out of here.'

'Break an arm,' ordered Vince.

One of the two men suddenly twisted Kenser's left arm violently, and with a sickening crack heard above his screaming it snapped at the elbow.

As his screams subsided into sobs, Vince spoke again. 'Now you understand, Kenser Donnelly, that I mean business. Speak only when spoken to. Do you understand?'

'Yes, yes,' gasped Kenser.

'Right,' continued Vince, 'you've been brought here on two charges.' He was acting the judge now. 'Charge one of rape, and charge two of murder.'

Kenser stared towards us, tearful and mystified, but afraid to speak. I glanced at Vince, who was staring back at him, his jaw set as he tried to contain himself, his anger showing through the hard exterior. 'In June 1963 you raped a schoolgirl called . . .' He looked at me with his eyebrows raised.

'Marilyn Wisheart,' I said aloud. 'At 4.35. In the French rooms.' I don't know why I said that. Nervousness maybe. But it seemed to add weight to what I was saying.

'You raped a schoolgirl called Marilyn Wisheart,' continued Vince. 'What do you say to that?'

Kenser hesitated, grimacing with pain. 'Everyone was at it. She was just an old slag.'

'That's not true!' I shouted. 'She came down into the basement cloakrooms for a bit of fun, and it all got out of hand when you turned up. I saw it. I saw you come into the room and shag her while the crowd held her down.'

Still shackled by pain from his broken arm, Kenser offered his explanation. 'It's what she was after, you know that. It's what they all wanted.'

'Like fuck,' I said. 'You fucking raped her! She asked you to stop and you just carried on!'

He tried to see past the lights. 'Who are you, anyway?'

'Never mind who we are,' interjected Vince. 'As I see it, you're guilty. Anybody disagree?'

There was a silence, marred only by the whirring of the camera and the shifting of Teddy.

'Listen!' shouted Kenser suddenly. 'Whatever happened, I didn't mean to upset the girl.'

Vince stared at him for a few seconds before speaking. 'You're going to find out what that poor girl went through, you scumbag.' He glanced at Teddy and nodded towards Kenser. Then he looked at me. 'You don't have to stay for this,' he said softly.

I took a deep breath. I guessed what was coming but didn't know if I could stomach watching it. Kenser was standing waiting, wondering, his eyes wide open with undisguised fear, and despite the animosity I felt towards him, I couldn't prevent a feeling of revulsion for his predicament from bubbling to the surface. Then I thought of Marilyn Wisheart and the look of agony on her face. 'Get on with it,' I said.

At a nod from Vince, the two men in white forced Kenser face down over the butcher's block. Struggling was out of the question with his arm broken.

Teddy approached him silently, carrying his bag, which he placed on the floor, then quickly strapped Kenser's legs to those of the butcher's block before he had a chance to resist. He then stood back to consider Kenser's rear. 'How do you want this done,' he asked, looking back at Vince. 'With a bit of artistry, or . . .'

'Just do it!' snapped Vince, looking away.

So he was uneasy too. That made me feel a bit better.

Teddy unfastened Kenser's jeans and pulled them down, with his underpants, to just above his knees, as far as they would go. At this Kenser began bellowing. 'What the fuck are you doing, you cunts? Leave me alone!' Then he began crying aloud, wailing; it was a strange noise from a grown man.

Silently, Teddy delved into his bag, put on rubber gloves and began rubbing cream from a tube all around and into Kenser's arsehole. I glanced at Vince, but he was looking away.

Teddy seemed to be getting agitated, his breath coming in short bursts as he worked, then suddenly he pulled down his own strides and I saw what Vince had meant earlier. I couldn't see how it was going to work.

As Kenser blubbered, his face down on the slab, Teddy positioned himself and gestured to one of the men in white to twist his broken arm. Kenser screamed, first from the pain in his arm, then from the pain as Teddy took him from behind. Like a dog, he lunged into Kenser – who by now seemed to have passed out – until he finally arched his back and grunted as he reached the end of his performance. Then he quickly withdrew, standing back with the practised flourish of a matador as Kenser's bowels emptied on to the floor. With casual efficiency, he then cleaned himself up with cloths and lotions from his bag before pulling his trousers back up and rejoining us.

I stared at him with horrified fascination. This was one very nasty person.

'Okay,' said Vince, suddenly businesslike. 'Teddy, I'll catch up with you later, all right?'

Teddy, his job done, was now almost starchy, offhand, like he'd suddenly lost interest. 'Okay, can I make a call from reception?'

'Speak to Ray. He'll sort you out.' As Teddy left, Vince turned his attention to Aitch. 'Have you got enough, or do you want to see it through to the end?'

Now what were they going to do? These geezers were so fucking clinical.

Kenser was being revived by the men in white, who were splashing water on him.

'What we've got so far's all right in the right market, but if you really want some interest we'd be better off shooting the lot,' replied Aitch. 'We'll mask the face out, of course, unless you particularly want it left in.'

Vince turned to face Kenser. 'The second charge is one of murder; murder of my little brother . . .'

Kenser, released from the ankle straps but now standing with his trousers and underpants around his ankles, began to cry again when he realised his trial wasn't over. 'I'm sorry, I'm sorry, I really am sorry, please don't hurt me any more. I can't take any more.'

Vince turned to me. 'What do you reckon, guilty or not guilty?'

'I reckon he's had enough,' I said. I had.

'Guilty or not guilty?' he persisted.

'I don't know, do I? I wasn't there. I can't truthfully say who exactly did it.' If the truth be known, I wanted Vince to let Kenser go. He'd been reduced to a sub-human and would never be the same Kenser Donnelly again. And hurting him any more wasn't going to bring Dinger back. 'I think he's had enough – why not let him go?'

But Vince ignored that suggestion.

Looking back at Kenser, he said, 'Taking into account the fact that your friends who were with you when you drowned my little brother in the sea at Brighton all said independently that it was you who held him under despite their pleas for you to stop; taking into account the fact that you ran to the States afterwards – which indicates guilt; and taking into account your character and previous record, I say you are guilty. Good fucking riddance. Do your stuff, boys.' He shifted in his seat and looked at me as if to say 'This is what happens when you cross Vincent Bell'.

Without a moment's hesitation, one of the two men in white took a slaughterer's stun gun from a pocket in his overalls, placed it quickly against Kenser's temple and pulled the trigger. Kenser's knees gave way as the bolt pierced his brain, and he crashed to the floor like a puppet with severed strings, his legs kicking impotently of their own accord.

And despite everything, I hadn't been expecting this. Just how do you expect something you've never experienced before: the quivering and twitching of the limbs as the nerves die; the final release of body waste as the corpse relaxes?

They removed his boots and socks, picked him up and hung him upside-down on a hook by both Achilles tendons. Then, using sharp knives, they cut off his clothes. Working fast, as skilled butchers do, they cut his throat, drenching the floor with blood, opened him from groin to chest and pulled his guts out with a splat on to the floor. Then they ran the carcass out of the room on the overhead rails.

My head swam, and I thought for a moment I was going to lose it, but fear of being unconscious in that terrible place stopped me.

'What are they going to do with him?' I asked Vince weakly, feeling salty juices gushing into my mouth.

'Dog food,' was all he said. Then he got up and walked out.

Next to me, Aitch, entirely unaffected by events, was finishing off the filming as if he'd been taking a holiday movie. Then, after carefully packing the bits and pieces away in a box, he folded the tripod, put it in with the rest, closed the lid, slung it over his shoulder, said 'See you around' and left.

Apart from four chairs, the butcher's block, four leather belts and a steaming pile of guts, I was alone.

A cold wave of dread swept through me as I glimpsed momentarily the immensity of what I'd just witnessed. Where did I go from here? Freedom for me was a thing of the past; I was an accessory to Vince's harsh sense of justice, one of Kenser Donnelly's murderers.

'Tommy! Change your clothes and put them in the incinerator.' It was Vince again.

'Oh . . . yeah . . . where is it?' I stood up shakily as the men in white reappeared to remove the guts. Using rubber-bladed sweepers, they pushed the grisly heap out of the room, then returned to hose the place down.

And Kenser was gone, out of my life forever.

That night, back in the flat, I lay awake with the light on, trying to hide, listening to the night noises coming from the crowds of innocent unsuspecting lucky bastards outside. I tossed from side to side, afraid to close my eyes and see again the images of horror that had branded themselves into my brain. But even with my eyes open they flooded back, and I had to force myself to study objects within the room to maintain a concentration that would keep my mind from turning towards Kenser and that terrible white-tiled room.

I stood up and began to pace around the tiny flat. What were my options now?

I would have to carry on working for Vince, hoping that nothing ever came of the Kenser mystery – after all, sooner or later someone would notice he was missing.

And what if the film got into the wrong hands? Or someone found a toenail in their dog's breakfast?

Surely Vince would have to be number-one suspect in any investigation into his disappearance?

Which brings me neatly into it. Life for murder.

And what if the photographer decided to blow it when he fell out with Vince? Or Teddy the queer? Or Ray the minder? Or the men in white? There'd have to be more killing. And I'd have to help, otherwise I'd be the next one for dog food.

I was sweating now.

I could run to the Old Bill. Turn Queen's Evidence.

Fuck that. I'd have no pride left at all then. Everyone hates a grass, even the Old Bill, despite what they say. And life would be worse, having to hide like a fucking cockroach for the rest of my life.

I could kill everyone able to identify me. Very funny. Out of the question.

I could commit suicide.

I sat down again.

Or I could level with Vince, tell him I'm not made for

this sort of stuff. Tell him I'm moving out of the area and getting a job – why didn't I listen to my old man? I would have been well on my way to being a technician by now. Safe. And innocent.

Or I could just disappear without saying anything to anyone. Trouble with that is my family. Unless I clear it with Vince, he might start bothering them, even if it's only to find out if I'm all right. I'd have to clear it with him first.

That's it. I'll carry on for a while and save money. Then I'll tell Vince I want out – to go and start a new life in New Zealand. I'll tell my mother and my old man the same thing. Then I'll fuck off and travel around the world forever.

Unable to bear my own company for another minute, I jumped off the bed, slipped some shoes on and went out. Still gripped by my imagination, I ran down three flights of stairs and out into Lexington Street, up to Broadwick Street, then left into Carnaby Street before I realised what I was doing. Crossing over the road, I walked into the Roaring Twenties.

Stoneface was on the door as usual, and I swear he almost smiled, which cheered me up a bit. He must have seen some terrible things in his time. I could hear Count Suckle's sound system down below pounding out ska music, and I felt the knife-edge fear in my gut beginning to lift. I just hoped someone was there I could talk to.

Downstairs was busy, but apart from a few regulars I vaguely knew, there wasn't a soul from the usual crowd. I went and sat by the stage with a bottle of Coke topped up with rum and tried to switch off, letting the rhythm wash through my mind.

'The higher the monkey climb
The more he expose . . .'

Some time later, I saw Frankie walk in alone. He looked pissed off. But seeing me he grinned, went straight to the bar for two rum and Cokes and came to sit next to me, handing over one of the bottles. For a while we just sat grooving silently to the music, letting the rum do its work, but being so close to the stage and speakers it was impossible to talk and it seemed he had something to say, so we moved to the back of the club where we could hear each other.

'I'm fucking sick of this place,' he said as soon as we'd made ourselves comfortable.

'The Twenties?'

'No, London. England.'

'Yeah, I know what you mean. Me too.'

We sat drinking and watching the dancing for a few minutes as a tall, lithe black sort danced with a black geezer old enough to be her granddad.

Frankie suddenly looked at me. 'D'you fancy coming abroad, travelling about, you know what I mean, just bumming about from place to place?'

This was incredible. 'You're joking . . .' I said, staring at him to see if there were any signs he might not mean what he was saying, like wildly dilated pupils.

'I'm fucking not. I've been taking a long look at things, and all the signposts are pointing to fucking Doomsday unless I take a big jump on to another track. I mean it, Tommy. There's no fucking hope for me here in this shithole.'

I laughed aloud, not with humour but with joy. Frankie looked bemused. 'I'm laughing because I've come to the same conclusion,' I said. 'I'm going next spring. To Europe, Africa, the Middle East, I don't fucking know, anywhere.'

Frankie beamed. I'd never seen him look so pleased about anything. 'It's about time you got away from that mob you're working for anyway, before you get too tangled up with them. You want to watch that Vince, he's right fucking dodgy – I mean, big time.'

Too tangled up – that's a joke. I wonder if murder counts. 'That's what I was thinking,' I said.

And we clinked bottles just as 'Madness' came on . . .

ELEVEN

BERYL THE PERIL

Although I'd spent many sleepless nights trying to work out how to make a clean break from Vince's organisation without any comebacks, threats or commitments, the solution arose suddenly and unexpectedly, just as I was beginning to think I had little option but to disappear.

As another sharp English winter arrived, I'd taken to socialising with Frankie and acquaintances of his around south-east London rather than getting involved any more than was necessary with Vince and his mates, and between dreaming of warmer climes and getting pissed up, I'd begun seeing a woman fifteen years older than myself who I'd met at one of Frankie's parties.

She'd been quiet all night, sitting to one side as everyone talked about ruling the world, and it was only later on, after she'd poured more than enough alcohol down her neck, that she began putting herself about. For some reason everyone was very polite to her but, ignoring them, she eventually drifted over and asked if I fancied a dance. About the same height as me in her heels, with the platinum-blonde bouffant hair that east London women of that age seemed to prefer, she had a nice face, despite too much eye make-up, and kept her figure well.

I was indulging in her Chanel No.5 and the pressure of her left tit against the back of my right hand as the Four Tops sang 'Baby I Need Your Loving' when she put her pale-pink glossy lips to my ear and whispered, 'Do you fancy getting out of here?'

'Sure,' I said. 'What's your name? Mine's Tommy.'

'Beryl – and don't laugh. Pleased to meet you.'

Beryl the Peril. I hope not.

Five minutes later we were shagging in a pissy lift between floors while I kept the lift at a standstill with one finger on the 'stop' button.

From there we drove back to my little flat and screwed all night, with only one interruption when Vince called to collect cash. Throwing on my strides, I kept him outside and explained quickly that I was with my girlfriend and that she was very shy about meeting strangers under such circumstances, and I hoped he didn't mind doing business on the landing, but that's the way it was. He was fine.

'Just make sure you don't go getting the poor girl into trouble,' he said with a smirk.

When I went back in, Beryl was as white as the sheet she was clutching about her neck. 'Who was that?' she asked. 'I recognised his voice.'

'Who was it then?' I challenged.

'I'd recognise that voice anywhere. Vince. Vince Bell.' She stared ahead at the wall.

'How come you know him then?'

'My old man works with him.'

Her old man. Fuck. I had the feeling someone like her wouldn't be single but had sort of dismissed it, assuming that they'd split up or something convenient. But this was even better. It gave everything an air of indecency and I wanted to shag her again. 'So?' I said carelessly, sitting down on the edge of the bed.

She hesitated. 'Are you working for Vince, then?' Her eyes looked worried, almost frightened.

'Yeah,' I said. 'Why?'

'Shit!' she gasped, 'For Christ's sake don't tell him you

know me. It's a good job he didn't come in! If this gets back to my old man we're both dead.'

I laughed, trying to appear unconcerned. 'Don't worry about it. I'm not going to say anything, am I?'

'It'd be the last thing you did,' she said.

I pulled my trousers off again and rolled back next to her, aided by the dip in the old bed. I kissed her cheek. 'Who's your old man?' I asked. 'Do I know him?'

It turned out he was one of Vince's closest associates, Ray Skinner – someone everyone respected for being shrewd, a sort of second in command who kept a low profile, planning future operations. Good job he couldn't see me now, playing with his old lady's clout. She was getting breathless again.

There was a danger, of course. If he found out, I was dead, or at least badly damaged. There was no doubt about that after what I'd seen. She could well be too, although I thought he'd be more inclined to let her see what had happened to me, just to warn her about straying again. And Vince would be unlikely to help because he was a strong family man, hypocritical bastard. Her hand found my cock again and I could feel those bright-red nails dig in as she ran her fingers slowly up and down. Fuck it. It was my birthday in a couple of days anyway – what more could a young bloke want? Despite the risks, life could be wonderful sometimes.

But I was beginning to dislike Vince and his organisation more and more. They terrorised people – a lot of them people I quite liked – then went on about morals and codes of living and how you should lead your life, what you should and shouldn't do. It didn't matter to him that Sheila, for example, was brown bread now, because she was a *freelance* tom and had to expect that as a risk – like the other six who'd been found chopped up over the last year or so. It didn't matter that one of the boys from Lewisham had the mentality of a five-year-old after his battering, because he was 'out of line'. And the shot geezer – he was married. What about him? And *his* old lady?

'What do you do when you work for Vince then?' she whispered absent-mindedly.

We shifted position and began screwing again.

'Collect rents, mainly, although sometimes I have to go out on special jobs.'

'Like murdering people . . .' She opened her eyes and stared at me. Surely she hadn't heard about Kenser?

I laughed. 'You're joking. Sometimes they go somewhere team-handed to put someone right about something, and I have to go with them. But usually it's just collecting rent.'

'Protection money, you mean,' she said, half closing her eyes again.

'Yeah, I suppose so.'

'Doesn't it bother you?'

'Sometimes.' The old bed was beginning to creak. 'Doesn't it bother you being married to him?' I'd only met Ray a couple of times but it was clear he had a lot of influence. In fact, there had been times when I'd wondered if he was Vince's boss.

She opened her eyes wider. 'I hate him. And I hate all the blokes he mixes with. When I first met him I thought he was one of the boys – smart, good-looking and all the rest – but he's just a mean bastard, a cheat, who don't give tuppence for me or anyone else, except as a personal possession.'

I slowed down a bit, wondering how to guide the conversation away from the subject. If we weren't careful she'd turn herself off. But after a little while she closed her eyes and smiled. 'I'm glad I met you – I feel like I'm getting my own back on him.'

I had to try hard to avoid feeling that I was being used and concentrated instead on the idea of shagging someone's woman behind their back, something I found disturbingly erotic. 'I tell you what,' I said, beginning to push home a bit harder. 'Let's be really naughty and shag each other silly for a while until we think it's time to cool it. No strings. No attachments. Just . . . lots of this.' The bed began creaking again.

'It's a deal,' she whispered.

Everything went fine for nearly three months while the winter months peaked and began to wane towards spring. Cherry blossom was beginning to appear in uplifting bursts of whiteness throughout the damp London streets, again urging my mind towards ideas of escape and another way of life.

We met in different hotels from time to time as the urge grabbed us and might have carried on indefinitely but for the fact we were seen together one day when we decided to take a risk and use my flat again after we'd failed to find a room somewhere else. As we were climbing the stairs, Vince ran straight into us on his way down.

He looked at me, then Beryl, then me again, and his mouth dropped open. Beryl just froze.

'Tommy?' he managed to stammer. I'd never seen him lost for words before. 'Beryl. I, er, didn't know you two knew each other.'

My mind raced. I burst into a beaming smile. 'Do you two know each other?' I asked incredulously. I looked at Beryl. 'You know Vince?'

There was a tiny glare, a threat, in her eyes as she looked back. 'Yes,' she said, 'I know Vince.' She stared defiantly at him. 'Don't I, Vince?'

Vince was still lost for words. Finally, he looked down

and began to manoeuvre around us on the stairs. 'Well, I've got to be off,' he said. 'I'll see you later, Tommy.' Then down he went without looking back. 'Oh, and take care,' he added. 'It's bad luck to pass on the stairs.' Then he was gone.

After he'd gone, Beryl became hysterical. 'Ray'll kill me, he'll kill me!' she screamed. 'I don't believe it – I knew we shouldn't have come back here. Shit! Oh my God, what are we going to do? Don't just stand there, say something!'

I grabbed her shoulders and forced her to look at me, because that's what they do in films. 'Listen! Listen! Nothing's going to happen. Don't worry.'

'And you!' she screamed, pushing my arms away. 'Talk about look after number one!'

'What are you going on about?'

'The way you said,' she put on a prissy face, '"Do you two know each other?" As if it was all down to me. I couldn't believe my ears! How could you? After all we've agreed to.'

What else could I have said? Anyway, we hadn't agreed to anything except 'no ties' and 'no commitments', but now it had come to the crunch she was losing it; if I didn't cool it she might invent all sorts of rubbish to get herself off the hook. 'Listen to me. Listen!' I shouted.

She quietened down.

'Me and Vince go back a long way. I went to school with his little brother – we were best mates. There's no way he's going to say anything to drop me or you in it. There's no point. It won't do him any favours at all. The worst that's going to happen is that he'll give me a bollocking. Anyway, all we were doing was walking up the stairs; it's not as if he caught us at it.'

'I was hardly coming back to your flat to look at your etchings, was I?' she said scornfully.

I laughed again, trying to lighten things up. 'I know that. But all I'm saying is that no one knows what's been going on – we've just been lucky, that's all. I'll tell him we met for the first time somewhere today, and I was just showing you where I lived. Then he turned up and you wanted to go home in case he got the wrong idea about us.'

'I don't know. Where can we say we met? I'm supposed to be at home.'

'Anywhere. I'll say I stopped you in the street because I thought you were someone else, and we got chatting. We had a coffee . . .'

'And I agreed to come back to your flat. Sounds great. Beryl the slag. Entices boys off the street for lurid sex sessions.'

'Hold on, I'm twenty-one.'

'And the rest.'

'Look, whatever you say, Vince will not tell your old man, I promise.' I wasn't too sure about that, but what was the point in frightening her any more? The main thing was to get myself off the hook. 'I'll talk him out of anything, and anyway, as I said, he's got nothing to gain by grassing on you.'

She looked away. 'Until they all fall out.'

Naturally she was right. If I knew Vince at all, this knowledge would just serve as a tool to be used when it suited him.

I put my arm around her shoulders. 'The worst thing is, we're going to have to call it a day, you and me.'

She looked up sharply. 'Why? What's the point in stopping now? If Vince keeps his mouth shut, so what? If he doesn't, we're dead, so we might as well enjoy ourselves while we can.'

This female was crazy. But I could see her point of view. On the other hand, I had no intention of dying yet, so a meeting with Vince would probably be a wise move. 'Look,' I said, 'Vince could come back any moment, so I think we should get this sorted out first. You go home and forget me for a couple of weeks, and I'll get things straight with Vince. If everything's okay I'll leave a card in the window in Danny's newsagent's saying "Flat to Let. Single bed requires occupant", nothing else. Okay?'

'Then what?'

'Well, if you still want to see me, leave a card saying "Single girl seeks single-bed flat". Put a time and a date on it, and I'll meet you in the Whispering Gallery in St Paul's.'

'What if things aren't okay?'

I shrugged. 'No card. Just keep your head down and invent some story to cover yourself. Just remember, apart from meeting Vince today, nobody knows anything, so tell them anything.'

'But what are you going to tell Vince?' she asked.

I thought about it. 'I know,' I said. 'I'll put a card in the window advertising for a part-time secretary. I've been moaning to Vince that I need someone to keep the books. That's it!'

Her face suddenly softened. 'Yes! That's it! I've been going on about looking for a job as well, but he wouldn't let me – that would explain why I looked so worried when we met Vince!'

'There you go. And you've had to turn me down now that you've found out I work for Vince. Perfect.'

Then she looked all sort of dodgy. 'Not at all. I think I'll accept the job. If you clear it with Vince we'll have the best of both worlds.'

'But he'll talk to your old man then.'

'Exactly. And if he thinks I'm working for the firm, he'll probably say yes.' She began to undo my shirt. 'And if I do a little bit of overtime, who's going to know?'

I grabbed her hand. 'You're a fucking nympho. Listen,' I said, doing up my shirt again, 'if Vince was to come back now we'd blow it. Go home. I'll speak to him tonight about the job, all right?'

'Spoilsport,' she said. Then she pecked me on the mouth and left.

To tell you the truth, she was beginning to get on my nerves. The sex bit had been all right – especially when she went down on me. I'd never had that before. Even Monica wouldn't do that because she'd said it was 'demeaning' and something 'psychologically perverse' that males needed, whatever that meant. But the first time Beryl did it I thought I was going to faint. And that's all I wanted for a while until the novelty wore off. But she was definitely beginning to get on my nerves now; I wanted to get back among the virgins.

Vince sat and listened to my spiel about looking for a secretary until at last he appeared satisfied with the explanation. When I'd first walked into his room he'd looked as if he was ready to tear me apart, but I managed to handle the psyching-out bit and cheerily got into the swing of lying through my teeth, going on about how much of a coincidence it was that he knew Beryl, and did he think his partner would mind if she worked as my secretary, and how difficult it was getting to remember who I'd collected from, and how maths wasn't my best subject and so on, until finally he agreed to discuss the matter with Beryl's old man.

I was still worried about whether they'd believe the incredible coincidence of her applying for a job with me, but Vince seemed to sense this and said, 'I'll tell him we need a book-keeper and suggest Beryl, saying that we need someone we know and can trust to do the job.' He stared me in the eye. 'I don't think he'd believe your story, do you?'

210

I had to admit that it defied belief. Then I wondered why I was bothering to go along with this at all. All we needed was to make sure Vince wasn't going to break the news of our stairway meeting. And he wasn't. Now I was going to get lumbered with a secretary who would have me by the balls mentally and physically the moment she walked through the door.

'What's up?' asked Vince. He could see I looked uncomfortable.

I didn't know where to start. He might not be so understanding if he knew that I'd been fucking his mate's wife for the past three months. As it stood, at least he had something to cling to, no matter how dubious. If I told him everything, he might just lose his rag. 'I don't know, Vince,' I said. 'To be quite honest with you, and please don't take this the wrong way, but before I knew who she was, I thought she'd make quite a tasty secretary, you know what I mean?' I hesitated for effect. 'But her being who she is and all that, I'd rather find someone else.'

'We need someone we can trust. What's the problem with Beryl, then? Do you think she's going to be too much to handle?'

'I thought she might be a bit of fun to try it on with. But now I know who she is, no way. You know what I mean, Vince? There's no way I want to rock the boat.'

He stared long and hard at me, and when he finally spoke I discovered that I was as taut as a drumskin. 'I *don't* know what you mean, Tommy. In fact, everything you've ever said to me has been said in such a way that it could be taken to mean almost anything. You're probably one of the craftiest monkeys I've ever set eyes on, and to be honest I'm still not sure whether I like you very much. I took you on because you were the friend of my little brother, and for a while I believed that I'd made the right choice, that in some daft way you might be able to take his place, but then Monica came along and you fed me that line about her freelancing . . .'

'But that was . . .'

'Shut up Tommy. But I gave you the benefit of the doubt. I thought she'd do you a bit of good. Maybe help you grow up a bit. And then there's the odd pound or two here and there that goes missing.' He stared even harder, waiting for me to deny it, but I couldn't. 'And then there's all this silly Mod and Rocker business, this running riot down the coast at Brighton and Margate or Hastings or wherever it is, and I think to myself, who is this person? I wanted someone who was straight, who told me the truth, who realised that he had a good future in front of him. But what have I got? A little tearaway, running around like a dog with two dicks, whose life is in utter fucking confusion. Someone who is entirely unreliable – no, that's not true – *unpredictable*, except where women are concerned, and lacking in loyalty. Now you come here asking me to overlook the fact that you've been sniffing around Beryl, my mate's wife. Come on, Tommy, don't treat me like a complete cunt.'

The funny thing here was, he was right – and wrong. Sure, I'd shag anything given half the chance, but isn't that what blokes are about? The money was out of order, okay, and maybe I was unpredictable, but as far as I'm concerned unpredictability means strength. As for the Mod and Rocker thing, well, it was a laugh while it lasted, but all the others had knocked the arse out of it. And as for Beryl, she'd pulled me; I didn't know her from Adam, or should I say Eve?

'You're right out of order, Vince. I agree that I owe you money, and I'll square up next week. As for the rest, well, the trouble is you don't understand what's happening any

212

more. Don't tell me you wouldn't shag a bird if she came on to you . . .'

'Not my best friend's wife.'

He was a dodgy cunt.

'I didn't shag my best friend's wife. And don't try to twist it that I've been shagging this Beryl, either. I told you, I wanted a secretary – okay, a shaggable one – but when I found out who she was, no way. By the way, don't tell her I thought that.'

'Believe you me, the whole thing stays right here.'

'Thank fuck for that. As I was saying, you don't understand people younger than yourself. Everything's changed. I look at you sometimes and I see my old man, demanding, always demanding. You want me to do this, you want me to do that, and you expect me to live my life according to your rules, but I can't. Can't you see that? Ever since I was born I've been fed shit by people who've tried to use me to their own ends: family, teachers, police, the people I've worked for, including you, and I'm sick of it.'

He fucking clapped. He sat there and clapped, just as I was about to burst into tears. At my age.

'You're just the same as all the rest,' he said. 'All you do is fucking whinge and moan, criticise other people, blame them for your fuck-ups . . .'

'I'm not blaming anyone. I'm telling you the way I see it and you don't like it. Come on, admit it. And you do sound just like my old man. As soon as someone points the finger and says you're doing it all wrong, you say they're moaning and blaming someone. You're no better than these so-called pillars of society, who bleed everyone dry when they've done with their noble fucking words. You're just at the opposite end of the scale to them, but still bleeding dry anyone who's enough of a cunt to put up with it.'

Vince looked bored. 'The world's not a perfect place,

Tommy, and I never took you for a philosopher, but . . .'
Suddenly he had that mad look in his eyes again. 'Let me
tell you, if you don't *take* in this life, you'll starve. And I'm
not saying take from your friends. I'm saying take from the
others, anyone that's got more than they need, and hang on
to it with every ounce of strength you have. This is the law
of survival. Ignore it at your peril.' He paused to eyeball me.
'And don't preach to me. You've got a lot to learn. You threw
away the idea of working legally for a living when you
realised you didn't have enough to offer for the amount of
income you wanted, so after a bit of petty thieving you
came to me. And you've done all right for yourself, don't say
you haven't. Now you're getting out of control, getting big
ideas, and as much as I try to accommodate you, saying to
myself "he's still young", what do I get? A fucking preacher.'

'Who told you I was into thieving?'

He laughed. 'Here you go again. You haven't got a clue,
have you? When someone starts rolling old geezers on our
patch we get to know about it. You came very close to getting yourself in trouble, but lucky for you my little brother
was your partner in crime. Shame about the slag.'

There was a long silence as I took in what he said. This
was yet another side to the Vince I thought I knew. He had
no sympathy for Sheila at all, and I thought he was the big
white knight when it came to the opposite sex.

I considered my position now. Our working relationship was obviously over, which didn't bother me as I'd saved
up enough to split off with. But would he let me go? Surely
I knew too much.

Once again, he seemed to read my mind. 'The problem
is, Tommy, I can't just let you go, you know that, so what
are we going to do?'

'Why can't I just go?'

'Don't be silly, Tommy. As I see it, you're going to have

to carry on under my wing, as it were – as much as I'd like you to move on.' He sat for a while, considering what to do, and when he finally spoke again, his voice had a vicious keenness to it. 'Listen carefully: you step out of line once more and you'll have to go, I'm sorry. You can work out for yourself exactly what that means.' He breathed heavily through his nose as if he was trying to control himself.

'Anyway,' he said, suddenly changing his attitude and trying to be chummy, 'who knows, maybe if you get your nose down we might even get on again.'

And so it was. I had no choice until something else turned up. Great believer in things turning up, me. So I worked quietly and efficiently, collecting money for the organisation, keeping out of the way, constantly on the lookout for an escape route. Beryl was taken on by the firm and installed in a little office in Wardour Street which kept her away from me most of the time, and Vince kept his distance, as if he wanted nothing to do with the storm that was almost certain to come.

And then one day, out of the blue, Ray Skinner came to see me.

There he stood, bold as brass, as I opened the door. 'Ray!' I gasped, with a welcoming smile. 'What brings you here?'

He didn't smile. 'Can I come in?' he asked.

'Sure thing.'

He walked in, glancing around, and I had a sudden sweat, wondering if there was anything incriminating lying around, but it looked clean as far as I could see. All it needed was a pair of Beryl's distinctive patterned stockings or a long-forgotten pair of her initialled drawers hanging over the back of a chair. Why she had them initialled I don't know. Maybe he bought them for her. 'This is a bit of a shithole, isn't it?' he growled. 'Is this the best Vince can do for you?'

I laughed, doing my best to stay cool. If he knew the score with me and Beryl he'd have come to the point already. The problem was, exactly what did he want? 'It suits me. Right in the middle of all the action.'

'"Action". Is that what you call it?' He sat in the one hard chair. 'Young geezer like you ought to be spreading his wings a bit. There's a big world out there, you know.'

What the fuck was he going on about?

He pulled a pack of Chesterfield cigarettes from his pocket and offered me one, which I took, then produced a gold lighter from a waistcoat pocket and lit us both up. He seemed a bit uneasy, so I offered to make a cup of tea, then realised the milk had turned into something nasty in the bottle.

'It's okay,' he said, spitting a piece of tobacco out and releasing smoke through his nostrils. 'I've just had a drink.' There was another long silence, then he began to speak as if preoccupied. 'Tommy, I don't know if you are aware of the extent and importance of our business operations . . .'

I sat on the edge of the bed and eyed him up and down while he was distracted. He was quite a sharp bloke, really, in his dark-blue chalkstripe cashmere suit and black brogues; they went with his neat black hair, although I thought his nose was maybe just a bit too small to put him in the handsome bracket. Then I thought of Beryl again, sucking my dick.

'. . . but they spread their fingers worldwide and involve thousands of people, from one-man-band capers to factories employing hundreds of people. Because of our organisation, thousands of people stay in work, their kids get fed, the economies of small and not-so-small countries remain stable, the leaders keep their heads on their shoulders and their comfortable way of life, and everyone's happy.'

Just what the fuck was he going on about?

'In this country alone,' he continued, 'we have direct links not only with thousands of commercial enterprises but also with investment enterprises in the City, some sections of the civil service and the police force. We have influential investors who rely on us to take care of their money, and their circle of friends include some of the most powerful people in the land.'

'I didn't realise the . . . organisation . . . was that big,' I ventured, trying to sound interested, 'or that these, er, top people were involved in it.'

'Most of them don't know either. But to put it in a nutshell, we're big, we're doing well, and we don't want any fuck-ups. Which brings me back to why I'm sitting here talking to you.'

He's sussed me.

I waited, ready to fight like I'd never fought before. The bottle of sour milk would have to do. Why didn't I keep myself tooled up? If I can get to it, I'll smash it on the iron gas ring and poke the sharp bit in his neck. Unless he's carrying a gun.

I wonder what it's like to be shot.

'Go on,' I said.

He breathed in deeply through his little snout. 'Vince has got to go. He's become a liability.'

I could have kissed him. Trying to keep a straight face, I asked why and where I came into it. Why was he telling me this?

'We're closing down his department, and you're part of it, that's why.'

Despite me wanting out, it still came as a shock to be told I was no longer wanted. A sort of blow to my pride.

And how could they get rid of Vince with all the knowledge he had in his head? Surely he had the organisation by the balls? 'But you'll still need someone to collect for you. Couldn't I carry on doing that? It don't bother me if Vince's going.' I hadn't planned on leaving this quick.

His eyes took on a mean look. 'Having gone through the books carefully, it appears that your accounting's a bit slapdash, so just consider yourself lucky we're going to leave it at that. Your new secretary's good at figures, so she'll be taking over.'

'Beryl?'

He stood up. 'That's right. Beryl. As I say, consider yourself lucky we're going to leave it at that. Be out of here within the hour. I don't want to see you again.'

With that he buttoned his jacket, turned and walked out.

Now what?

TWELVE

VINCE'S PROBLEM

Ray was true to his word. Vince left the organisation all right, but in a way I hadn't expected. When I first heard the news that he had been found dead in his car, shot through the head, I knew it wasn't suicide. For a start, the weapon used was a rifle; I mean, who carries a rifle into the busiest part of London to commit suicide? Talk sense. But that was the official view.

And after the little meeting with Ray Skinner I had a fair idea what had happened, so one day I went along to see Beryl to see what I could find out. As I expected, she was shocked to see me again.

'Tommy! What are you doing here?' she gasped.

I looked around at the office: a desk, two chairs, a typewriter and an adding machine, a black telephone and a picture on the wall of a little boy with a tear rolling down his cheek. To one side an open door led into a small washroom. That was it. Not even a window.

'You'd be better off in nick,' I said. 'At least you'd have someone to talk to.'

'I hope no one comes round and catches you here,' she said.

'Why's that?'

'Because I had one hell of a job convincing Ray you and me weren't seeing each other as it is.'

She was still as tasty as ever, despite her lairy dress sense, and her nipples stood out through her pink cardigan.

'"Seeing each other" – that's one way of putting it.' I affected a laugh.

'So what are you doing round here?'

'I've come to take you out – for old times' sake.'

She looked at her watch. 'All right, where are we going?'

'You don't care, do you?'

'Not really,' she said. 'For what my life's worth now, there's not a lot of point worrying.'

'That bad?'

'Put it this way: I get up, come here, stare at the walls all day or read, go home, watch telly, go to bed. How about you?' She looked me up and down. 'I see you're going for the more casual look.'

I was wearing torn Levis and a polo shirt and an old pair of blue suede loafers, down at heel. To tell you the truth, the mood had changed: smart wasn't cool any more, and I'd even let my French crop grow out so that I had hair over my ears and down the back of my neck for the first time in my life. 'D'you like it, then?' I asked, not caring whether she did or not. Her views were null and void anyway, being the age she was.

'I preferred you in a suit. So where are we going? Wherever it is I'd better meet you there. Oh, and by the way, I've got some news to tell you.'

'What?' I hoped it was about Vince, because that was the main reason for my visit.

'I'll tell you when we get wherever we're going.'

'Suit yourself. Where do you fancy? Skylight bar?' I decided to test the water. 'We could get a room after.'

'Yeah, I know. Let's keep it simple for now – I've got an hour. How about the Mitre?'

I grinned. 'Okay. See you there in a quarter of an hour.'

The Mitre was busy, but not packed, with lunchtime office workers and a few builders – I was glad she'd chosen there because I was too scruffy for Park Lane. I ordered a pint of Guinness and found a table near the back of the pub. Beryl came in within minutes and found me after buying herself a tomato juice.

'I would have got that for you,' I said.

'It's okay. I was already there.' She took a sip. 'So what's this all about?' she asked.

'Ladies first.'

'No, come on. You came to see me.'

I took a mouthful of cold Guinness and swallowed it, feeling the bitter, creamy tang in my mouth. What was she going to tell me? It could only be to do with the organisation. Whatever, it would have to wait. 'I want to know about Vince,' I said.

She looked at me askance. 'Vince? What about him?'

'You must hear stuff. Who killed him?'

Her mouth dropped open. 'What do you mean, "who killed him"? He committed suicide, didn't he?'

'Oh, come on, everyone knows it wasn't suicide. I won't tell a soul – I just want to know for my own peace of mind.'

She lit a cigarette. 'If I did know who killed him . . . sorry, d'you want one?' She passed me hers and lit another. 'As I was saying, if I did know, which I don't, I wouldn't tell you anyway. I couldn't.'

'I thought as much. I knew it wasn't suicide.'

We sat in silence for a while. I remembered Ray's visit, his words: 'Vince has got to go. He's become a liability.'

'Why was Vince a liability?' I asked.

'Who said that?'

'Your old man when he came to see me.'

'Yeah, what happened when he came round?'

'He just came in and said they were closing Vince's department, including me, because he was becoming a liability.'

221

'Did he say anything about *us?*'

'You and me? No. Just to say that you would be running the accounts or something. But I think he'd sussed something, the way he looked at me when he mentioned your name.'

'He suspected all right.' She drew on her cigarette again. 'No, I don't know whether I should be telling you this, and you've got to promise me you won't tell anyone else . . .'

'Yeah, go on.'

'Vince had a problem with women.'

I sat there stunned as she told me how the police had been on to him for the murder of several girls, and how the organisation had topped him and made it look like suicide. He'd probably murdered Sheila, too.

'Time'll tell, I suppose,' I said, staring into my glass at the froth tidemarks. Funny the way your mind works: I began thinking about tree rings. The biggest gulp I'd taken was the sixth one, roughly about when Beryl came in.

'Time'll tell what?'

'Whether he really was the Canal Path Murderer. If the killing stops, well . . .'

'I see what you mean. No. He was the one all right. Ray had him followed after one of the girls' workmates came and told Ray she thought he was a nut-case.'

I could have told them that. 'What, did they catch him red-handed?'

'They disturbed him and the girl got away, but the police were already on to him by this time so they had to get rid of him. Now everyone's happy.'

'Except the girls' families, who'll never find out who did it.'

We allowed a silent moment of respect for the dead to pass.

'So what's the other news?' I asked, when I thought we'd been respectful enough.

'I'm pregnant,' she said.

'Congratulations. Is Ray happy about being a dad?'

'I doubt if he will be. It's yours,' she said, lighting another cigarette.

I met Frankie one bright spring morning on Victoria Station, and with pockets full of money and rucksacks on our backs, we boarded the Golden Arrow for Newhaven and Dieppe, our destination Paris.

We plodded on through the train, looking for a good place to sit, past the tourists and businessmen and foreigners, until a little way in front I saw what looked like the perfect place.

'Can you see what I can see?'

He looked ahead. There sat two unaccompanied girls. And very tasty ones at that. 'Sorties,' he said.

'Come on, let's see where they're going.'

We stopped by them.

'D'you mind if we sit here?' I asked, as politely as possible.

They both stared at us, wide-eyed. 'Comment?' said one. They were French.

'Nice of you to offer. Thank you very much,' I said, and dumped my rucksack next to theirs.